Blue Dragon-Girl
Flatorte

Elf Apothecary
Halkara

©Benio

Red Dragon-Girl
Laika

The Witch of the Highlands
Azusa

©Beni

Don't think I haven't **trained for this day!**

...You'll regret showing me **as much kindness as you did.**

I've Been Killing SLIMES for 300 Years and Maxed Out My Level ③

Kisetsu Morita

Illustration by Benio

YEN ON

NEW YORK

I've Been Killing SLIMES for 300 Years and Maxed Out My Level ❸

KISETSU MORITA

Translation by Jasmine Bernhardt

Cover art by Benio

SLIME TAOSHITE SANBYAKUNEN, SHIRANAIUCHINI
LEVEL MAX NI NATTEMASHITA vol. 3
Copyright © 2017 Kisetsu Morita
Illustrations copyright © 2017 Benio
All rights reserved.
Original Japanese edition published in 2017 by SB Creative Corp.

This English edition is published by arrangement with SB Creative Corp., Tokyo in care of Tuttle-Mori Agency, Inc., Tokyo.

English translation © 2018 by Yen Press, LLC

Yen On
1290 Avenue of the Americas
New York, NY 10104

Visit us at yenpress.com
facebook.com/yenpress
twitter.com/yenpress
yenpress.tumblr.com
instagram.com/yenpress

First Yen On Edition: December 2018

Yen On is an imprint of Yen Press, LLC.
The Yen On name and logo are trademarks of Yen Press, LLC.

Library of Congress Cataloging-in-Publication Data
Names: Morita, Kisetsu, author. | Benio, illustrator. | Engel, Taylor, translator. | Bernhardt, Jasmine, translator
Title: I've been killing slimes for 300 years and maxed out my level / Kisetsu Morita ; illustration by Benio ; translation by Taylor Engel ; translation by Jasmine Bernhardt.
Other titles: Slime taoshite sanbyakunen, shiranaiuchini level max ni nattemashita. English | I have been killing slimes for 300 years
Description: First Yen On edition. | New York : Yen On, 2018–
Identifiers: LCCN 2017059843 | ISBN 9780316448277 (v. 1 : pbk.) | ISBN 9780316448291 (v. 2 : pbk.) | ISBN 9781975329310 (v. 3 : pbk.)
Subjects: CYAC: Reincarnation—Fiction. | Witches—Fiction.
Classification: LCC PZ7.1.M6725 Iv 2018 | DDC [Fic]—dc23
LC record available at https://lccn.loc.gov/2017059843

ISBNs: 978-1-9753-2931-0 (paperback)
978-1-9753-2937-2 (ebook)

1 3 5 7 9 10 8 6 4 2

LSC-C

Printed in the United States of America

Contents

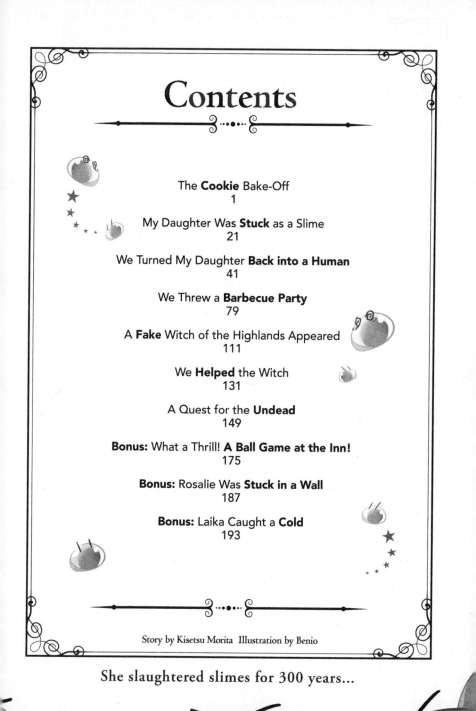

Story by Kisetsu Morita Illustration by Benio

She slaughtered slimes for 300 years...

Something was rocking me back and forth.

I felt a strange force, almost as though my body would be ripped in two. What could it be…?

When I opened my eyes, I found Falfa and Shalsha standing on either side of me, pulling me from side to side as I slept in bed.

But their swaying was out of sync, so they were either scrunching my insides or almost tearing me in half.

"Heave!"

"…Ho."

"Heave!"

"…H-ho."

Shalsha was a beat too late!

It's times like these I see how different they are, even if they do act so much like twins, I thought, but now wasn't the time to be overwhelmed by emotion.

"That hurts, so stop shaking me!"

"Oh, you're awake, Mommy!"

"Good, good."

Falfa beamed, and a slight smile appeared on Shalsha's lips.

Shalsha was still becoming more expressive by the day. She didn't used to smile at all.

"You were sleeping for a long time and didn't wake up, so we got worried and came to get you, Mommy."

"We already had breakfast. It's way past time to get up now."

Seriously? I looked at the clock and, sure enough, it was an hour and a half later than usual.

"Oh, I see... We did just come back from the demons' castle, after all..."

A lot—a whole heck of a lot—happened at the demons' castle, so it must have worn me out. I guess I was sleeping soundly now that I was in a familiar bed.

"Whose turn was it to make breakfast today? I don't think it was mine..."

We all took turns making meals here in the house in the highlands. I had a feeling it was supposed to be Laika's turn, but wouldn't she have woken me up properly?

I headed for the dining table and found a mound of cookies placed on it.

Well, more like piled high on it.

Two piles, each on a big plate.

What is this...? There's enough here to open a bakery... Are we going to have an eating contest...?

"Oh, good morning, Lady Azusa."

Laika looked exhausted, too, but that was probably mostly due to travel. To be honest, it would be weird if the trip hadn't worn her out.

"What are these cookies for, Laika? I mean, I wouldn't mind cookies for breakfast, though."

There was really nothing wrong with cookies, except that they could dry out your mouth. They seemed rather nutritious anyway.

"Actually, this is—"

A new face popped out from right behind Laika, cutting her off.

"Mistress, please try one of the cookies I made!"

The girl was Flatorte. Unlike Laika, who had only horns, Flatorte also had a tail in her human form, so she stood out like a sore thumb.

"I am sure the cookies I've made will be much better than Laika's!"

Flatorte tried to push her aside, but Laika similarly held her ground.

"Oh no, no. My cookies will be much better, because I am well aware of Lady Azusa's preferred tastes."

"Ha! Then she'd tell you they were good just to be polite!"

"How rude of you! That is the most despicable thing about you blue dragons!"

The two gritted their teeth and glared at each other.

Aah, their quarrel gave me the rundown on the situation. Now that I thought about it, they had been talking about having a showdown with sweets on the leviathan on our way home from the demon lands.

Oh. I'd thought they were just getting caught up in the moment, but I guess they actually went through with it.

"Okay. Then I'll decide whose is the most delicious, fair and square."

The two nodded, satisfied.

They matched better than you'd expect, didn't they? They were both dragons, so it wasn't that weird if they were perfectly in sync.

"Then I'll get Halkara, Falfa, and Shalsha, and all four of us will decide together whose is the bette—"

"We can't have that." "I agree."

They both refused. *They really are in sync.*

"I have focused all my energy into baking cookies that you will find delicious, mistress, so I want to see your reaction alone."

"I, too, have made them to suit your tastes, Lady Azusa. And if all four of you were to act as judges, then there's a possibility it would end in a draw."

©Benio

No matter what the outcome, one of them would end up holding a grudge…

I sat down, and they placed several of each cookie on two plates before me.

In order to keep it fair, I had no way of knowing who baked what.

"I know you will pick mine, mistress!"

"Victory is impossible for you, considering how long Lady Azusa and I have known each other!"

I wanted them to stop fighting, since it would only make it harder to savor the cookies…

Anyway, I started on my late breakfast. If they tasted good, then all would be well.

First, the right-hand plate.

"Ooh, it's buttery and the texture is very light. It's not bad at all."

I ate three in a row. It was a very high-quality cookie.

It would be easy for me to tell who baked it if either of them smiled, so they stood silently with meek expressions.

Next, the one on the left.

"This one has roasted beans mixed in with it. The texture of this one is quite interesting, too. It's almost like the sweet *senbei* we had in Japan, where carbonated water was mixed into the dough."

They were called *tansan senbei*—a thin, crispy, sweet cracker. I often received them as souvenirs from people who went to Arima hot spring.

"So, Lady Azusa, who is the victor? I believe it is me, of course."

Laika stood in front of me.

Her comment…made this much harder…

But still, though they both looked like cookies, the concepts were much different than I'd imagined. It was like having trouble giving an answer to the debate of which was better—math or language arts. It was hard to make a choice.

"Now, which is it? I know the winner is me!"

Flatorte confidently stepped before me as well.

Oh no, what to do...? I want to avoid giving an answer that isn't well thought out, and hurting someone's feelings... This would be much easier if one of them clearly tasted better than the other...

As I deliberated, the expressions on both their faces were brimming with confidence.

Smug, you could even say.

"This is clearly my victory."

"It's mine, *Flatorte's*, obviously. I've already got my victory shout prepared!"

Don't both of you announce your win like that!

It's getting way too hard to choose!

Oh well. They've left me with no choice but to use my secret move.

I stood up.

Both of them stared at me.

"And the winner is—both of you, since they were both so delicious!"

It was too hard to pick a winner, so I fled from the choice with all my might!

This is fine! It's totally fair! I chose the path with the least sadness! And I really was having a hard time making a decision!

"Lady Azusa, you can't do that..."

"Mistress, you may be as merciless as you please here."

Neither one was satisfied, after all. No, no, this was no time to be ruthless.

"This extremely haughty individual ought to cry. It would be perfect karma."

"Excuse me, *this* individual is acting all high-and-mighty only because she's lived here for a long time. Could you please shut her up?"

"That's what I'm saying! It's almost impossible to choose because both of you keep spouting nonsense like that!"

I wanted them to put themselves in my shoes for a second.

"And even though they're supposed to be cookies, they're clearly different concepts. You would have a hard time, too, if you were asked to choose between an omelet or fried chicken, wouldn't you?"

"I would choose an omelet."

"As would I."

That was a bad example.

I knew Laika liked omelets, though. Were there lots of omelet fans among dragons?

Either way, I knew they weren't happy with a draw, so I thought of a countermeasure.

"Well, why don't you sell the cookies in Flatta and decide the winner by who sells the most?"

The two stared blankly at me, as though my suggestion was beyond anything they could have expected.

"See, it's hard for an individual to choose on their own because the flavors are so different, but it'd be easy to come to a conclusion through sales, right? Why don't you decide the winner that way?"

"If you say so, mistress, then I have no objections."

"My victory over you will be overwhelming, and I will show you how much more skilled I am!"

Thankfully, I escaped ending up as the bad guy.

And there was another advantage to this method.

Flatorte was now a new member of the family, and I was waiting for an opportunity to introduce her to all of Flatta.

Selling her homemade cookies would make for an excellent first impression.

$$\Diamond$$

That day at noon, I went to the village and gained permission from the chief to use an empty building.

However, since many people in the village went shopping in the morning and stayed inside in the afternoon, we decided to hold the competition the following day.

The two also needed to make more to sell, so it worked well with our schedule.

And I'll take the chance to tell you now that the cookies that were like sweet *senbei* with roasted beans were Laika's cookies. They were apparently originally invented in a hot springs area by a volcano, so they might actually have the same origin as the *senbei* sold around hot springs areas in Japan.

The next day, we opened the Witch's House cookie shop in Flatta.

But although the shop had only one name, the cookie sales were calculated separately. They were sold by the bag.

"Welcome! These cookies are much more delicious than the ones beside them!"

"Try these cookies! They're so much more delicious than the ones over there, it would be stupid to compare them!"

Could they at least stop dissing each other while advertising their cookies?

Now I had no responsibilities, so I relaxed and watched on.

By the by, Rosalie the ghost was floating near the sale stand as the referee, making sure that neither of them played any dirty tricks.

I didn't think either of them would, but she was also there to make sure the loser didn't accuse the other of an unfair win. They were both sore losers, so it was possible.

"Bohh of 'em rea-hee are goooooood, 'ough."

Halkara bought one bag of each type of cookie. She was stuffing her face as she talked, so it was hard to understand her.

Falfa and Shalsha were also taking cookies from the bags and munching on them.

"Falfa is so lucky to have more snacks!"

"That's great, Falfa. They should make some for us more often."

There were very few people at first, but the people of Flatta tended to flock around any new rumor, so the crowd gradually got thicker.

"Ooh, we get cookies this time from the great Witch's House?" "Which one should I get? I guess I'll get both." "Great, I'll get one of each, too!"

Both types were flying off the shelves.

And I thought I saw more male customers, despite the product for sale being cookies.

"Laika's the cutest one, though." "The new girl's like a big-sister type. I like it." "Ooh, you going for her?" "You were always a fan of Halkara, though!"

I see, so they were popular like idols in a way. There were only girls in my house, after all.

But there was also a line of girls acting the same way.

"I'd want Laika to be my little sister." "She's way too cunning. I'd want someone like the new girl." "But doesn't a tail mean *she's* the cunning one?" "I like it, even if it does. I could stroke her tail as her big sister to calm her down."

The world sure is full of interesting people…

The two *were* cute, so their popularity wasn't odd.

In terms of outward appearances, Laika looked like she had just entered middle school. On the other hand, Flatorte looked a little older, somewhere between middle and high school.

From my perspective, it felt like my two little sisters were scrambling for my favor, so it wasn't all that bad.

"Oh, Madam Teacher, that was a vulgar look on your face just now."

Ack, Halkara pointed it out. *She really didn't need to see that…*

"It's the same face I make when I'm calculating that month's sales."

"Wait, you do it, too?"

"You know, I'd say that the addition of Flatorte was a good incentive for Laika, don't you think?" Halkara commented as she watched the two sell their cookies.

Of course, she was also in the middle of a match, but Laika's expression certainly looked livelier than usual.

"You really like to observe, don't you?"

"I was just thinking that if we added some ground herbs to the dough, we could sell it as a wholesome snack to the health-conscious demographic."

"For *business*?!"

But it probably really was good for them to have someone to compete against.

Sometimes people talked about competing against themselves, but that rarely ever happened. It was much more common for people to cut themselves too much slack.

So it was easier if the enemy was an outside force.

I'd just likened them to sisters earlier, and that wasn't entirely off base.

And by the way, the cookies were being received very well. I heard several comments from the villagers:

"The cookies we bought were so good, my kids told me to go buy some more!" "I gave them a taste test, and I am definitely buying them!"

I knew for sure they would do well when I ate them yesterday.

And just as the last cookie disappeared from Halkara's bag—

"Well, I'm getting back in line to buy one more bag each."

"Get two, Big Sister Halkara!"

Falfa announced her demands.

We sure were buying a lot of them ourselves…

The two had made quite a lot, likely because they were so confident, so their product remained on the table into the evening despite how much they were selling.

It was just before nightfall.

The last customer bought one bag each, and the competition was over.

"They both sold out at the same time, too."

"That doesn't matter; there's no point unless they're competing to see who makes more money. If it was who sold out the fastest, then the one who made the least would be at an advantage."

They both sold their cookies for three hundred gold per unit. That was about three hundred Japanese yen. The price was the same, so whoever sold the most would also be ahead in amounts of money.

"There was no foul play during the time of sale. I, Rosalie, have kept careful watch."

Rosalie the judge announced there were no violations of the rules, so we would now start counting revenue.

"I believe I can calculate the fastest, so I will count."

Halkara quickly lined up the bronze and silver coins as she counted them. As a merchant, she worked very quickly.

The two competitors gulped as they watched on.

"I will not lose. The village of Flatta is counting on me as well."

"It's not like they acknowledge you as a professional cookie baker. When it comes to quality, you are no match for the great Flatorte."

"By the way, was there supposed to be a special benefit for the victor?"

"Now that you mention it, I don't think we decided on one... Why don't we pick one now...?"

The two started mumbling about something.

Wouldn't the loser just get a flick to the forehead at most?

For some reason, a mass of townspeople started to gather by the shop. It seemed like everyone was interested to see who would win.

In the crowd, I could see banners with messages like, GOOD LUCK, FLATORTE! and GLORY IS YOURS, LAIKA! If these people could turn something into a festival, they would do it right away...

"All right, I've calculated the revenue. The price for each was the same, so I will announce the number sold."

When Halkara spoke, everyone looked to her, not just the competing duo.

"First, Laika—three hundred units!"

The townspeople cooed, "Wow!" I was surprised, too. The town's population was definitely less than three hundred, which meant quite a number of people had bought multiples.

"That many? I hadn't paid attention to how many I was baking."

Laika admitted the truth. She had made way too much, thinking about it generally.

"The great Flatorte never thinks about the *numbers*. I knew a good thing would sell, so I trusted in that."

Both of them seemed satisfied with how things were turning out.

"And now, for Flatorte."

Everyone looked to Halkara.

The two competitors obviously couldn't relax, and they both wore prayerlike expressions.

Who would be the victor?

For some reason, Halkara smiled joyfully just before delivering the answer.

"Can you believe it—three hundred units! Which means it's a tie!"

Of all things!

That must have been the most entertaining result for the spectators, since there came an excited "Oooohhh!"

It was like a high school baseball match, where both teams' pitchers were throwing strikeouts and the match had to be rescheduled, since no one was winning!

The two looked at each other.

"What should we do now...?"

"As she said, it's a tie. It's just the same as before..."

In a way, I was happy that my conclusion that they were both equal was validated.

I stood between the two and lifted one of each of their arms in the air.

"We have two winners! Please give them a warm cheer and round of applause!" I called, and clapping broke out in response. There was even someone playing a flute.

"And this girl is a new member of my household, Flatorte the blue dragon! Please treat her well!"

There was another cheer.

I could hear things like, "Welcome!" and, "Flatta's a great place!"

"Oh, mistress, did you actually plan all this...?"

It seemed that Flatorte finally caught on to my plot.

"Indeed. Don't you think it's the perfect opportunity for Flatta to accept you?"

I hadn't thought of too many details for it to be called a "plan," but my relationship with Flatta had lasted for three hundred years so far. Our bond of trust was strong. So even throwing something together would still bring great results.

Flatorte's eyes glistened with tears.

"I was worried about starting a new life, but...I knew you were great, mistress... Fantastically great!"

Flatorte hugged me on the spot. It was a powerful embrace, since she was a blue dragon, but my status was unfairly high, so I managed.

"Come now, no need to cry."

"I will stay with you for the rest of my life, mistress!"

This girl was more of a clingy one than I thought. Maybe she had been used to putting up a strong front before.

"Hey, that's against the rules! You can't do that!"

For some reason, Laika protested. She should let the newcomer do what she needed to for now, especially since Flatorte truly felt so anxious.

But something about what she said caught my attention.

"What do you mean, 'against the rules'?"

"The rule was that the winner of this challenge would be allowed to hug you, Lady Azusa, for ten minutes."

What? This is the first I'm hearing of this... I did not consent to this... And that's too long. Ten minutes is too long.

But there was no doubting that they'd both worked really hard, so afterward, I gave a big hug to Laika, too.

◇

That night, the population density in my bedroom increased a bit. And my bed itself was a little crowded, but what could I do?

Laika and Flatorte were on either side of me.

"Now then, let's get along when we sleep, like the roman numeral three."

"The what?"

"I don't know, either."

Oh right, I was thinking of my old life. And that would imply we were all the same size.

"All of us sleeping in one bed like this makes us seem like sisters, right? So going by height, I'd be the oldest, Flatorte's the second oldest, Laika's the youngest, and all three of us are supposed to get along. Okay?"

"I understand, mistress…" "I will follow your orders, Lady Azusa…"

"Okay then, tonight, we sleep together!"

Feeling blessed, I fell straight to sleep and dreamed of having a delightful cup of tea at a café with my two sisters.

"*Yaaawn…* I slept so well!"

I had a very pleasant night, but it didn't seem the two on either side of me did.

"I didn't sleep a wink…"

"Me neither…"

Apparently, neither of them got to sleep.

"Was the bed too narrow for you…? If it was, then I'm sorry."

"No… I couldn't calm myself when I thought about how I was in the same bed as you… And, mistress, you smelled so nice…"

"I was so, so happy, I felt like sleeping would be such a waste of time. So I stayed up…"

Both of them sure were making a big deal out of this.

"If you want, I suppose we could do this once a month or so."

To be honest, it was easier to do things like this now that Flatorte had joined us.

Up until recently, I wanted a way to draw a clear line somewhere when it came to sleeping with Laika, since I am a woman of age, of course, and even though we were of the same gender.

But with the three of us, it was more like a sleepover, so I felt my resistance lessen.

"Oh really?! Do you really mean that?!"

"You're overreacting, Flatorte..."

Her tail was whipping to and fro... That thing really had a mind of its own. It was way different from a cat's tail.

"Indeed. You need to be more, you know, ladylike..."

Laika's face was bright red, too, as she spoke, though...

Ah, I knew it. The younger sisters both look up to the eldest.

Then, I was surprised to see Laika yawn.

"Once preparations for tomorrow are over, I think I'll head to bed early tonight..."

"I agree... For once, I agree with you..."

Flatorte seemed pretty sleepy as well.

"Hmm? What preparations for tomorrow?"

I thought I was supposed to be in charge of making food today.

"Lady Azusa, the cookies have proven to be extremely popular, so for the next while, we will be making them every other day."

That often?!

Oh no. I didn't think they'd be that well received. It was supposed to be a one-day-only deal.

"And by the way, it seems we'll be selling in the town of Nascúte tomorrow. We'll need to prepare today. I didn't sleep very much, but I'll do my be— *Yaaawn...*"

Flatorte gave a big yawn, too.

Feeling somewhat responsible, I decided to help make and sell them.

◇

The day we brought the cookies to town, we sold much more than we had in the village.

Frankly, we made so much money we could live off these cookies.

"Can you imagine if we produced them en masse and sold them throughout the country?" said Halkara. "It'd be amazing!" She sounded like a CEO.

"No. Each individual cookie must be made with love and care, otherwise they won't be good."

"Only the great Flatorte can make her magnificent cookies. It won't taste the same from the hands of another."

Both of them sounded like professionals.

"Madam Teacher, don't you think some weird switch has been flipped in them? They are acting like cookie-baking professionals, aren't they?"

"They sure do look like they have thirty years' experience..."

From then on, the cookies sold very well. Maybe too well.

We got a request to open up shop in the provincial capital of Vitamei, and after that, more and more people began associating dragons with cookies throughout our province.

And then we returned to Flatta again and for one day sold cookies there.

"Madam Teacher, it really is getting to be too much..." Halkara was staring at the line leading out the front of the shop.

"I know. Say what you will, but they are really getting burnt out..."

Exhaustion was starting to catch up to the two dragons after several days of work in a row.

But the more they made, the more they sold, so they just kept on making.

"We have to stop them sometime, otherwise they'll collapse... I don't think dragons die from overwork, though..."

"Yes... We should probably intervene at some point..."

But a little while after opening sales, something strange happened to the air about town. And the clear skies suddenly clouded over.

"Oh dear, I'm getting a chill…"

Halkara started shivering.

I, too, felt an ominous presence.

"Long time no see, Sister."

The girl with sheep horns on her head was the demon king, Provato Pecora Ariés, also known as Pecora.

Beside her was Beelzebub, holding a parasol above her to protect her from the sun.

There was also Vania the leviathan, holding out another parasol—it was like a *matryoshka* of parasols.

"Aah! Why did you come here?!"

"I heard this was where those extremely popular cookies were being sold, so I came to have a taste. By way of leviathan."

Oh! I thought it had suddenly gotten cloudy—that was the leviathan! Since Vania was in human form, then that meant everyone had hitched a ride on her older sister, Fatla.

"There is always trouble when Her Majesty travels, so I really wish we didn't…" Beelzebub sighed.

"I—I pray this will all go smoothly…" Vania seemed frightened, probably because she was traveling with the demon king.

"Eh-he-he-he, so we should line up, yes? I suppose it wouldn't be too terrible to join a queue like a commoner every once in a while."

Pecora then politely went to the end of the line.

But even the most common of commoners seemed to understand the terror of the demon king.

"H-hey… There are demons behind me!" "I thought something was in the air, and turns out it was a giant demon!" "The legendary leviathan!"

The villagers were frightened. Some of them may have been acquainted with Beelzebub, but it seemed the leviathan had a big impact on them.

Then, Pecora spoke to the villagers with a smile.

"A pleasure to make your acquaintance! I am the demon king."

"It's the demon king!!!" "It's the end of the world!!!" "What are we gonna do now?!?!" "O great Witch of the Highlands, please defeat the demon king!!!"

All those waiting turned pale and ran off.

The line shrank to about ten people in an instant.

Or from a different perspective, there were ten whole people who *weren't* going to run away?

"Oh, well, now we can make our purchase quickly. Wonderful."

Pecora seemed excited by her sudden stroke of luck, but I knew her ulterior motives.

"You scared off the villagers to put yourself at the front, didn't you...? I bet that's why you came on a leviathan, too."

"I don't quite understand what you mean, Sister."

You sure look *like you know what I mean!*

This demon king is always up to something...

On the other hand, now with fewer customers, Flatorte and Laika stared on blankly in amazement.

"I think we can carry the rest of the inventory back, but what should we do, Laika...?"

"Oh dear, I don't know..."

Though Pecora ended up buying all the remaining stock, the cookies now had the reputation of attracting the demon king, so we had significantly less people asking us to make more.

Pecora's arrival did cause us trouble, but the two were finally freed from a long stretch of work, so I suppose all's well that ends well.

I was sure we could go into the village once a month or so for a more relaxed little sale.

AZUSA AIZAWA

The protagonist. Commonly known as "the Witch of the Highlands." A girl (?) who was reincarnated as an immortal witch with the appearance of a seventeen year old. Before she knew what was happening, she'd become the strongest being in the world. Although she's had some rough times, it has ultimately given her a family, and she's delighted about it.

PERSE-VERANCE EQUALS POWER. I ONLY DO THINGS I CAN STICK WITH!

LAIKA

A dragon girl and Azusa's apprentice. She's fastidious and cares a lot about what others think, but she's a good, earnest, hardworking girl. Gothic Lolita clothes, maid outfits, and other frilly things suit her very well (which embarrasses her).

LADY AZUSA, I'LL DEVOTE MYSELF TO IMPROVING AGAIN TODAY!

The cookie commotion died down, and the house in the highlands was quiet once again.

The morning sun streaming in through the window woke me up.

"Oh, right. It's my turn to cook today. I need to get ready."

Just as I was going to leave my room...

Bang, bang, bang! Bang, bang, bang! Bang, bang, bang!

There was a loud and forceful knock on the door.

What on earth did this person want?

"O-oh no! Oh no! Mom, Mom!"

The voice belonged to Shalsha. It was so loud and animated compared to normal, I almost thought it wasn't her. But now wasn't the time to admire her courage. Something strange was going on!

"What is it, Shalsha?!"

I opened the door and there was Shalsha, sniffling.

Oh no—did she and her sister fight? It didn't seem so, though.

"...*Sniff*... *Hic!* I don't know...what to do..."

She reached out to hug me, but I still had no idea what happened.

"Calm down, Shalsha. I can't tell what's going on, now can I?"

"Sister... My sister..."

"Did you get in a fight with Falfa?"

"No..."

Which meant her older sister hadn't done something terrible to make her cry.

In that case, then a slightly terrifying possibility came to mind.

"Did something happen *to* Falfa?"

Shalsha still seemed shaken, but she nodded.

We couldn't stay sitting here for long.

I left the room immediately.

Shalsha's reaction was too much for something like catching a simple cold. I didn't want to think about it, but could something even worse be happening?

"Falfa, what is going on?!"

And there was something sitting in the hallway that shouldn't be.

A big blue slime, bouncing up and down.

The longer I stared at it, the more I wanted to eat *warabimochi*, but this wasn't the time for such carelessness.

"Why is there a slime in the house? We need to kill it."

The slime must've come in the same way a bug ends up inside. I didn't know how slimes thought.

Shalsha immediately ran up behind me.

She wrapped her arms around me tightly, trying to stop me.

"No, Mom! No!"

"Why? Were you researching this slime?"

"That's…my sister."

……

…………

"Sorry, I don't think I understand."

"When she woke up this morning, she was a slime…"

No way. It was just a regular slime, no matter how hard I looked at it.

The slime was bounding its way toward us.

Then, it nestled close to me.

At the very least, it didn't seem like it was planning to attack. I mean, I didn't know if that was the right call, but from its behavior, it looked like it was playing instead of attacking.

I'd heard that the strength of slimes depended on the RPG they came from, but at least in this world, they were the weakest monsters.

"Hey, are you really Falfa?"

Boing, boing.

The rather big slime bounced.

I had no basis to judge whether this was an expression of confirmation or not, but it did feel like she was saying *yes*.

"Wh-what should we do…?"

With no other ideas, I gave it a pat. In response, it swayed side to side. I guess that meant it was happy. The way it moved was different from other wild slimes.

"It got happy when I gave it a pat, so I guess it really is Falfa…"

It was a mystery, since there was no precedent for this.

"Shalsha, can you tell me more?"

Nod, nod, nod. Shalsha's head moved more than it usually would.

"When I woke up this morning, my big sister looked like a slime… The window was closed, so it's impossible that one snuck in from the outside. Slimes can't open doors, so it couldn't have come in from the front door. So the only conclusion is that the slime is my big sister…"

How mysterious. But if she was in her room the whole morning, then there was a good possibility it was true. It wasn't like a slime was going to emerge from the ground.

"Shalsha, you know a lot about slimes, don't you? I'm not saying you do just because you're a slime spirit, but you wrote a dissertation thingie about them before."

That's right, Shalsha was also a young genius—she had a serious researcher side to her.

"Would you know a cause or solution? It's beyond me, at the very least…"

"What I researched was purely anthropological. I'm no better than a layman when it comes to biology…"

Oh, so it was different. There was probably a big difference in the cultural and scientific side to things.

I looked at (the slime I thought might be) Falfa.

Yep, that was a slime.

"This is a family emergency, so let's get everyone together and talk for now."

And so the family convened.

It would be a problem if someone saw slime-Falfa before hearing an explanation and defeated her, so we decided to keep Falfa in the room and explain outside it.

After that was over, we moved to the dining room.

Slime-Falfa followed.

She couldn't talk, but evidently, she somehow still had her personality.

"Now we'll begin the meeting to save Falfa... Please raise your hand if you actually do know how to solve this problem."

It wasn't out of the question for the problem to be unexpectedly simple.

For example, like when the home-page screen suddenly gets really big and you start to panic because you can't close it at all, but it turns out that all you had to do was press the F11 key.

Or like when you get confused because you're on the overwrite mode.

All my memories were of computers... I still had them even after three hundred years.

There were plenty of things in the world that weren't a problem if you knew what was going on but nigh impossible to deal with if you didn't.

"Does anyone know how to cure slime form?"

No raised hands.

This was an unusual situation, after all.

"Then...I am now accepting ideas of things you want to try."

"Ooh, Big Sis, pick me!" Rosalie the ghost raised her hand. "This is where we pray really hard that she'll turn back, right? They say those who believe will be saved!"

It was very surreal hearing a ghost say that…

But this was a world where magic and ghosts were just everyday things. It would be too hasty to laugh off the possibility that prayer could be effective.

"Very well, then. Rosalie, use an empty room to give your prayers."

"Okay! I will pray my hardest to save my big sis's daughter!"

Even though Rosalie would be doing all she could, I still wanted ideas. Something more specific, preferably.

"Lady Azusa, wouldn't magic help somewhat?"

"I don't really think I can create such unique spells on my own… Oh, but we can ask Beelzebub about demons."

I started casting a spell.

"Vosanosanonnjishidow veiani enlira!"

It was the spell that summoned Beelzebub. This was an emergency, so I didn't hesitate to use it.

Splash!

A sound came from the bathroom.

Beelzebub was here.

Water dripped from Beelzebub as she emerged from the bathroom.

"Hey… Your pronunciation was a bit off, so I ended up in the wrong spot… I mean, I hardly mind if it's a little mistake, but you could at least drain the tub… The same thing happened last time…"

Sorry, but I'll have to deal with your complaints later.

"We need help, Beelzebub! Falfa turned into a slime!"

"You called me all the way out here for a foolish joke?! And a really terrible one at that!"

"It's a very terrible reality."

I held slime-Falfa in my arms and showed it to her.

"This is Falfa."

"…But this *is* a joke, right?"

"I would've had the mind to empty the tub if it was a joke."

The color suddenly drained from Beelzebub's face, and she immediately snatched slime-Falfa from me and squeezed tightly.

"Ooh, Falfa, look what's happened to you… Why would someone do such an awful thing to you?!"

"It probably isn't anyone's doing. She was suddenly like this when we woke up this morning. Is there any way to turn her back to normal?"

The Falfa-looking slime wiggled about in Beelzebub's arms. I wasn't exactly sure what that was supposed to signify…

"I mean, you may ask me that, but Falfa and Shalsha are already oddities among oddities. I doubt there's any precedent for this…"

"But still, slimes are monsters, so that would be your jurisdiction and not humans', right? Can't you do something…?"

I was planning on having Shalsha ask a slime researcher, but I didn't think they could prescribe a solution, since this was so new. Beelzebub was our only hope.

Beelzebub buried her face in Falfa (probably) to think. I wasn't sure if she was able to breathe.

"Okay. Every monster knows its own business best, after all!"

That sounded like the idiom, *Every man knows his own business best.*

"We should ask a slime about slimes."

"You mean, we could ask a slime and learn something that way…?"

I didn't think catching any number of slimes in the area would give us useful information. Unless there was some sort of machine in this world that let us know what creatures like dogs and cats were thinking.

"There's one that's very special, the Smart Slime in Vanzeld Castle."

"Wow… Of course something like that would be in the demon capital… So what is this slime's name?"

"The Smart Slime."

"No, I mean the proper noun. I mean, I'm sure it is wise among slimes."

"The Smart Slime *is* its proper name. You don't find smart slimes very often, after all."

"I dunno, that name doesn't really make it sound that intelligent…"

I had my doubts, but we needed to give it a chance.

◇

Slime-Falfa and I mounted Laika in her dragon form and headed for Vanzeld Castle. Now was not the time to take a leisurely flight on a leviathan.

Never in my wildest dreams did I think we'd be visiting demon territory again so soon…

We meandered through the mazelike castle.

"The Smart Slime looks for quiet environments, so it'll probably be on the lowest floor in the castle. That's where we'll head."

Beelzebub walked farther and farther ahead.

We made countless turns left and right in the hallway and went down steps leading underground.

Just as I was starting to get impressed that we weren't lost in such a complicated place, Beelzebub's expression clouded over.

"What…? Was there a path like this on the third basement floor…?"

"You don't know where we're going, either?!"

"I am clueless on the paths I don't use for work… But we will be fine. I've been dropping bread crumbs as we go, so heading back will be a cinch."

However, slime-Falfa was busy absorbing the crumbs one by one as she went.

Wow, this is my first time seeing a slime eat, I thought to myself, but that wasn't the question now.

"Hey! Falfa! You shouldn't eat things off the floor, remember?! When did your manners get so terrible?"

"Lady Azusa, please calm down! Now is not the time to scold her about manners!"

She was right. The fact that we were lost in a maze was the bigger problem.

And since we were on the third basement level, the path was awfully dark.

Before us was a creepy-looking corridor. This would be a great place for a test of courage.

"No need to worry. We may be lost, but we're still inside the castle. It'll work out soon enough."

"That is true. Oh, there's a map affixed to the wall here."

Laika had made an excellent discovery. Now we could pinpoint where our destination was.

"Oh, that map's a bluff, meant to throw intruders into confusion. The actual paths are nothing like this."

"Stop making it sound like a dungeon!"

Falfa bounced to me, probably because she was tired.

"What is it? Do you want me to carry you?"

I could tell Falfa was moving her body up and down. It was probably safe to say she was nodding.

"If your shoulders get stiff from carrying her, then give her to me. I shall carry Falfa as long as she wants," Beelzebub said. She was pretty reliable, too.

Falfa wriggled around, so I suppose she was happy.

"Either way, we just need to keep going deeper, and we should get there."

"Okay. It's not like we'll run into any monsters, so let's make our way through slowly and carefully."

And so we again began our advance through the dungeon.

I'll get to the deepest part of the castle, no matter what!

Two hours later…

Inexplicably, we ended up outside.

"Gaah! Why?! I thought we were going down, but all the stairs are going up! This castle is stupidly complicated!"

Beelzebub was very angry with her workplace.

Right. In order to go up in this castle, we had to go down once before going back up. We wouldn't get to our destination if we just went straight up or straight down.

That being said, one could sometimes end up on the ground while changing paths going up. That was what had happened to us.

"So demons get frustrated with this design, too…"

The layout was probably made for an enemy attack, but getting lost in it was much more infuriating.

"Drat… I cannot believe we can't even get to where the one person who could give us a hint is… Maybe I got the first staircase down wrong…"

Then, an elegant-looking girl slowly approached us.

"Oh my, what are you all searching for?"

It was Pecora, the demon king.

"I am touched to see my elder sister again. Why don't you come say hello and give me a kiss on the cheek?"

There she was, asking for a kiss right off the bat. I wasn't in the mood.

I explained the whole turn of events.

"—So I want you to tell us where the Smart Slime is. If you do, then…sure, I'll give you a kiss on the cheek."

I placed an offer on the table.

"Then might I ask for payment in advance?"

Of course, the demon king drove a hard bargain.

"Well, it's not like I have anything to lose, so sure, I guess…"

I gave her a light kiss on the cheek.

For some reason, I was sensing jealousy from Laika as she watched on from the side, but was it just my imagination?

"Aah… A kiss from my elder sister; what a wonderful experience! I fear I may swoon on the spot and die. I almost feel like a student at an all-girls academy…"

Pecora sure did seem happy.

I wasn't exactly sure if everyone was always kissing one another at real all-girls schools, but it sounded like the case in the stories she was reading.

"Lady Azusa, you cannot kiss people so freely... It may cause us to run into trouble again...," Laika warned me.

I did know that getting too close with Pecora could make things complicated, though.

Still carrying Falfa, Beelzebub sighed. "I knew this was a scam."

Give me a break! I wouldn't have kissed her if you hadn't gotten us lost.

"So now will you tell us where this Smart Slime is?"

"The answer is nearby. Take a good look."

"Wait, what? Just a hint...? Just tell us the answer..."

"In that case, that'll be a long kiss on the lips."

Pecora smiled mischievously, placing her index finger on her lips. That wicked woman!

"Er, I think I'll pass..."

I felt like if I indulged her too much, I could cross a point of no return and open a forbidden door.

"I'm not saying whatever I please, you know. Search long and hard. You'll find your answer. Well then, farewell, everybody."

And then she left just as leisurely as she'd come.

"So the answer is somewhere here... But there's no staircase going down. We're outside..."

"Wait. If what Her Majesty said was true, then the answer should be nearby..."

Beelzebub scanned the garden around her, and her gaze stopped on a small storage shed.

"...Could that be it?"

She rushed to the shed. Inside lay farming tools and the like. Just storage.

"No, that's not it. Let's search somewhere else."

"Wait, something smells," Beelzebub said and began poking at the ground.

Then, she discovered a floor panel that popped out. Beneath it was a staircase that led underground.

"This must be it! This is the path to the Smart Slime!"

"We would've never been able to get there with this!"

I really wish they'd cut the complicated dungeon-esque tricks!

The stairs leading down went pretty deep. It would've been pitch-black had I not used my Flame magic as a light.

"Lady Azusa, I find myself growing more and more fearful..."

Even though Laika was a dragon, it sounded like she didn't handle this kind of atmosphere well. It was probably like a pro wrestler being afraid of ghosts, so it wasn't that unusual.

"I'll protect you if anything happens, okay? Don't worry."

There was a door at the bottom of the stairs. At a glance, it was just ordinary wood.

"We made it. I never thought it would be here!" Beelzebub commented.

"I'm feeling very accomplished after all this work finding it, but we haven't solved anything yet," I said.

Beelzebub slowly opened the door.

Inside the room was a slime, almost two full sizes bigger than a normal one.

And its color was unique—practically pitch-black, like it'd been covered in squid ink. I'd never seen one like it before.

Inside was also the scent of mold and stacks of books. And some kind of scribbled writing on the wall.

It didn't seem very lived-in. But a human probably couldn't recognize a slime's daily routine anyway.

"Are you the Smart Slime?"

The slime leaped and hit the wall.

The word *Yes* was written there.

Beside it was *No*, and beside that was *Neither, I do not know,* and other words and phrases.

I see—this is how it communicates! It sure is smart! I won't argue with that!

"O Smart Slime, we are here because this slime-spirit girl suddenly reverted to her slime body one day. We thought you may know a way to solve this problem, so we came to you."

Again, the Smart Slime (from now on, abbreviated as SS) hit the *Yes*.

By now, it didn't seem so bad.

"This girl is like the bridge that ties slimes, humans, and demons together. Please help her. If you know a way, could you please tell us…?"

I understood Beelzebub's earnestness right away.

She was so concerned for Falfa.

As her mother, I was pleased.

Then, SS dragged its body across the floor to the opposite wall with several lines of individual letters.

Then, it started to jump over and over again.

"Could it be…trying to hit each letter to make up a word?!"

How advanced that is!

No, now was not the time to be impressed. I had to take notes to find out what it meant…

The first word was *wizard*.

In the middle of hitting the letters, SS must have misspelled something, because it even hit the spot that said *backspace*.

It sure was a dedicated way of communication.

And it was almost exactly like typing on a computer keyboard.

"Wizard. Slime. Tomriana Province. There. Mountain. Most. Tall. On. Should. Ask."

And putting it into a sentence would make—

"*You should ask the Wizard Slime that's on the tallest mountain in the Province of Tomriana*, right?!"

SS again moved to the *Yes* on the wall and hit it.

"A Wizard Slime… There sure are lots of different types of slimes, Lady Azusa."

"I'm shocked, too…"

Afterward, SS hit the wall a few more times to give us some additional information.

Apparently, some very intelligent slimes were born, and among those, some of them became SSes or WSes (short for Wizard Slime).

What the SS essentially said was that, since Falfa's physical body was the only thing that changed, we just needed to go to the WS and have it teach us the magic to return her body to normal.

Then I guess we're off to this Province of Tomriana.

We gave our sincere thanks to SS. Slimes knew slimes best, after all.

"By the way, what are you thinking about here?"

I didn't know the ecology of this slime very well, so I tentatively asked.

It answered, *I'm contemplating the meaning of existence.* And by *answered*, I mean it rammed itself against the wall to express words. It looked like a lot of work…

SS was incredible… To contemplate such philosophical concepts…

It also spelled out that its body had turned black because it was constantly hitting the wall. I never imagined such an impressive secret behind the color of its body!

"Thank you. I pray that your reflections deepen!"

Still in awe of SS, we left the underground room.

Now, our next destination was the Province of Tomriana, but Laika had already flown us here as a dragon and was starting to look rather tired.

"Laika, let's stay in Vanzeld Castle tonight."

"I'm sorry we're stopping because of me…"

"What are you talking about? You must take a proper rest after working hard—that's simple logic."

And I was tired, too. The shock of Falfa turning into a slime was nothing to sneeze at.

She might have originally been a slime, strictly speaking, but to me, Falfa wasn't a slime but one of my daughters.

Beelzebub prepared a room for us, so we decided to take a bath and relax for a while.

The rest of the family was probably still worrying about us, so I wanted to solve this problem as quickly as possible.

Then, something started banging against the door. I could tell it was Falfa by the rhythm of the bumps.

I opened the door, and Falfa hopped into the warm bathwater.

I couldn't have her sink too deep in the water, so I caught her with my hand.

"Do you want to take a bath, too, Falfa?"

She jumped in my hand.

Even in another form, she was still Falfa.

That brought me relief but, at the same time, a small bubble of sadness.

I wanted to free her from this situation as soon as possible. I wanted her to go back to the usual Falfa with the adorable smile.

"You just need to be patient for a little while longer, okay, Falfa?"

I gave her a big hug.

I could tell by the way she felt that this was Falfa, not just any old slime. I could feel her kindness through the embrace.

Even if she was lost in a whole horde of a hundred slimes, I knew I'd be able to find her right away by touch.

$$\diamondsuit$$

The next morning, Beelzebub came to our room.

"I did some research on the highest mountain in the Province of Tomriana. It's a very slim mountain called Mount Modadiana. Apparently, it's an environment where very few trees grow, and almost no humans enter."

"It sure does sound like we'll find something there. Thanks for checking it out."

"I would do anything for Falfa, as if she were my own daughter. I *will* help her!"

"I appreciate the sentiment, but she's my daughter, you know...?"

She had asked to adopt her in the past, so I wanted to be careful. I didn't know what I'd do if she ended up adopting away my kids one by one.

"Well, you have Shalsha, too, so you could just give one to me…"

So she is after them…! I can't let my guard down.

"It's not like giving you extra plates! They're twins, you know! I'd hate for them to be separated!"

"You're right. Then I'll take both."

Oh no. She doesn't get it…

We hopped on Laika in her dragon form and went to Mount Modadiana.

The mountain was indeed a desolate place, and there were no paths near the top.

Walking around and searching would be backbreakingly hard, so we split up to see if we could get an aerial view of a hut or some other wizardly residence.

Mages often had workshops in isolated places, so finding one here wouldn't be much of a surprise.

But looking from above, we couldn't find anything that could be it.

"We've flown around practically the whole mountain…," I said.

For the moment, we put our heads together to strategize.

"There's nothing growing here, so it's not like a forest is hiding it from view…," Beelzebub commented.

"We saw nothing that looked man-made to begin with… It's possible it might be living in a cave or something…," Laika offered.

"A cave, hmm? I can't deny the possibility— No, wait…"

Something Laika said jogged my memory.

"Beelzebub, can't you make a spell that detects magical power? If you can't, then I'll make it and master it myself."

I didn't think making it would be that difficult, but if someone else already knew how, then it would be much faster to have them do it.

"Aah, I see. I can do that. I'll give it a try."

It sounded like she understood my plan.

"Erm, what does that mean…?"

"Mages sometimes cast a glamour spell on their workshops to make them invisible to the naked eye. That might be why we haven't been able to find it after all this searching."

I knew these things, since I'd been a witch for such a long time. But in my case, I lived right out in the open in the highlands.

Beelzebub clearly seemed to feel something.

"I sense a quite powerful magic. It seems like there are a number of people there."

We headed straight in that direction, this time on foot.

"Lady Azusa, I didn't see anything around here before."

"Right, from the sky you didn't."

We kept walking, and eventually, a lone house suddenly appeared before us.

"Wow! I didn't know that was there."

"This way of hiding oneself is a basic trick for wizards. A poultice-making witch like me doesn't have as much use for this way of things."

The house sat precariously right at the edge of a cliff.

"Seems pretty typical. Shall we go, then?"

I knocked on the door of the little house.

After a moment, the door unlocked and opened, and there stood a "person."

She was a beautiful young girl of about fifteen years old, her blond hair braided up neatly.

The girl looked at her guests with surprise.

"Oh? And who might you be? It's quite unusual for people to come around these parts."

I was even more surprised. I thought another slime would come to greet us, but here was a person.

"Erm… Is this the Wizard Slime's workshop…?"

There was no one around here, so it wouldn't be entirely odd if other mages set up shop nearby.

"Oh, I see, I see. There's been some confusion."

The girl smiled brightly.

"I am the slime. This form is the result of using Transformation magic."

"*You're* the slime?!"

I couldn't believe my eyes. I mean, it was obvious, but I didn't see a single trace of slime anywhere.

It didn't seem like I was the only one with this reaction—both Beelzebub and Laika seemed to be questioning their whole reality.

"You're not trying to deceive us, are you…?"

"Of course not. I've lived three hundred years as a slime, but it's much easier to live in human form, so I've been living this way for about a hundred and fifty years so far."

Three hundred years old… We're practically the same age…

"Now that I think about it, I've never noticed any life span in slimes…"

I'd never seen an elderly slime or a baby slime, so I couldn't tell the difference at all. Both Falfa and Shalsha were spirits, really, so they were probably exceptions, too.

"The majority of slimes don't have proper intelligence, so life-and-death means nothing to them. They divide freely, and that's how their population increases. A very small number of them, like me, are intelligent."

"This is the first time I'm hearing all this, so there's no way I can verify any of it, but I guess I'll just generally accept it as truth…"

There probably wasn't any benefit to lying to us anyway.

"Oh, we'll be standing here talking for ages. Why don't you come in? Though, slimes don't really eat, so I have nothing to prepare tea with, and I don't have enough chairs, either."

We accepted her offer and went inside.

To be honest, it was pretty cold out on the mountaintop, so I was glad we could come in.

There was indeed only one chair, so we decided to stand and let her sit. The room itself looked and felt exactly like a wizard's workshop, with books filling the shelves.

It was a simple setup with just bookshelves and a chair—no toilet, no dining area, no bed. A slime didn't need any of those things.

Falfa was trying to eat bread crumbs, so she needed food, but I think she was able to get nutrition from most anything.

The girl called herself the Wizard Slime.

SS had been the same, so proper nouns didn't seem like something slimes cared much about.

"Almost nobody comes to visit my workshop, and they don't believe in Wizard Slimes anyway. I don't need another name."

I understood what she wanted to say, but we could see her as an actual person if she had a name.

"Then we can shorten Wizard Slime to make…wiz…slime… Okay, we'll call you Wizly."

The name sounded a little bit like someone forgot how to say *wisely*, but it would do, probably.

"Very well. Then please call me Wizly. So what brings you all here?" Wizly turned her gaze to Falfa. "I can tell that this has something to do with that slime over there."

Right. You're exactly right.

I told her that Falfa was a slime spirit, and then suddenly a slime one day.

"—So we're looking for a way to turn her back. Do you know how?"

"Hmm. Would you mind if I borrowed her?"

Falfa drew nearer to Wizly on her own.

Even in this form, it seemed like she still understood language.

Wizly lifted Falfa and started pressing points all over her body.

I guess it was similar to a type of medical examination.

"Hmm, I see. Her resiliency differs vastly from regular slimes, so there is no question that this is a special slime."

"You can tell?!" Laika was surprised.

"Yes. I can tell. I've been a slime for a long time, after all. To put it plainly, if we say regular slimes are at level one, then this slime would be about level thirty-five. Your average adventurer would have a difficult time defeating her," Wizly said, and I understood completely.

I had a hard time imagining Falfa and Shalsha having an even match with other slimes, and they did defeat them with ease in reality.

After that, Wizly kept poking at Falfa.

"Aah, I see. I see. Yes, mm-hmm, is that it? It is; it is!"

I wanted to interject, *What is?* But I figured there were some things that only slimes could tell...

Beelzebub spoke in amazement. "I've lived a long time, but the world is so filled with affairs I know nothing of." The slime world was deep.

In the end, Wizly spent about fifteen minutes poking at Falfa, then scribbling down some notes on a large dried leaf. I guess that was her replacement for paper.

"I have found an answer."

Wizly let Falfa go, and Falfa bounded her way back to me.

I caught her in my arms. "Please tell us! Please!"

We stood up straight out of respect.

"The reason this slime appears to be stuck in this form is because..."

"*Because?!*" I leaned forward.

What could it be? I hope it's not a bad omen...

"...she slept wrong."

""""*She slept wrong?!*""""

The cries of disbelief burst forth in unison.

"I never thought it'd be because she slept wrong..."

To be honest, it was a pretty stupid reason.

It was a relief to hear it wasn't the symptom of a serious disease, but I didn't think I'd hear such a run-of-the-mill answer.

"Yes, she did indeed. It's not a joke," Wizly said with a smile.

The way she said it suggested she was aware of how silly it sounded.

"This slime is typically in the form of a human, but she hurt herself when she slept in the wrong position. I understand that her body cramped up."

"So slimes get cramps, too..."

"Due to that, it became difficult to maintain her human form, so she turned into a slime. And because she was born in human form, she never knew how to change back. So she's been like this ever since."

I had never seen Falfa as a slime before, so "she doesn't know how to change back" was a pretty fitting answer.

"Then... Then how are we supposed to get the cute Falfa back?!" Beelzebub pressed.

"Instead of searching for a way to turn her back into a human, perhaps it would be more appropriate to say you are searching for a way to keep her human form."

To keep her human form...

I kind of get it, but I kind of don't...

"Demon, have you ever had trouble recognizing someone who usually wears heavy makeup without any?"

"Plenty of times."

Wow, so that happens to demons, too...

I'd thought how different some people looked without makeup, like on girls' trips and stuff.

"This is similar. This slime's human form was her makeup. And since she doesn't know how to do her makeup herself, she can't turn human again."

To me, makeup didn't seem powerful enough to make slimes look like humans, yet the metaphor was easy enough to understand.

But still, how were we supposed to make that a reality?

We could powder Falfa's face right now, but she would just become a powdered slime.

"Hmm, is there no quicker way? For example, couldn't you cast a Transformation spell on her to turn her into a human?" Beelzebub asked.

"Yes, I was wondering the exact same thing."

Once Falfa was in the form of a human and could hold a conversation, all would be back to normal.

"In theory, yes, but once the effects of transformative spells wear off, they must be cast again, and since transformative magic is *just* changing form, she will need training in order to, say, speak or write with her hands."

Sure. Her morphology would be that of a squishy slime that just *looked* like a human, so we couldn't expect her to speak. Even SS couldn't hold a conversation.

"But you're speaking and writing, aren't you, Wizly?"

"I had to practice for more than ten years to accomplish this. Even when I did change my form, my real self was that of a slime. I couldn't speak or write as much as I can now. It took me a whole month to be able to walk on two legs. Therefore, it's inefficient in many ways."

The more I heard, the more I understood how many problems there were with this solution.

"Additionally, since transformative magic turns the person in question into the form they envision, it's possible some parts of her could be different from before. She may be shorter than she used to be, or her expression could be different. Various discrepancies."

I got what she was saying.

They didn't even have photographs in this world, so it would probably be difficult for Falfa to be exactly as she had been before.

"Even my own face and body are completely different from what they were a hundred and fifty years ago. It's like an artist whose style changes as they draw."

Oh, so like that thing where the character images in a long-running manga look one way in the first volume and then totally different by volume twenty.

"I understand *very* well why it's no good. So why don't you tell us what the best possible thing for us to do would be?"

Beelzebub was being unusually forward. Emergencies like this always brought her kindness to the forefront.

"Of course. The quickest way would be for this slime to remember her own form and understand that is how she can return to her old self. In essence, it's not magic but shaping herself."

"And how should she shape herself?"

"In this case, it would be best to ask one who has kept a human form learning martial arts. You should ask for instruction from the Fighter Slime."

"The Fighter Slime?! That exists?!"

How deep did the slime rabbit hole go...?

"Yes. The Fighter Slime obtained its body through physical activity, not magic like I did. I believe you should learn the techniques from it."

So shortening the Fighter Slime's name would make it FS.

"So where will we find this Fighter Slime?"

Wizly's expression clouded over.

Wait, you don't know?!

"The Fighter Slime is always traveling the land in order to perfect its art, so it doesn't have a permanent address..."

"I can't believe this... It's way too much work to search the entire country... I'll have to make wanted posters like I did with Halkara..."

So we have to go stirring up panic again...?

"Oh, but the Fighter Slime always vows to train in the street and interact with others, so you may find it if you investigate town by town. It should also have a name for use in human society as well."

Phew! It had a name; that made this much easier! It would have been much too difficult to ask around after a slime-looking martial artist.

"Its name is actually Fighsly."

The naming style was practically the same as mine!

$$\diamond$$

And so we took the next step in our search.

We headed back to the house in the highlands to make flyers inquiring after Fighsly.

We also enlisted Flatorte to help, and we pasted them all over different towns.

Falfa's little sister, Shalsha, would be taking care of her until we found this Fighsly character. To be precise, she would put her in the bath to wash her and all that. "She's covered in dirt and dust, so we have to clean her," she'd apparently said. Well, Falfa was typically plopping along on the ground.

And when Shalsha brought vegetables to her for dinner, Falfa absorbed them into her body to digest.

It was unclear where her digestive system even was, but we could see whatever she had absorbed into her body slowly breaking apart, so she was eating.

"It doesn't have to be cooked food, because she can get nutrients

©Benio

from the dirt and weeds around her. That's why slimes grow everywhere. They hardly need anything like what we would call a meal."

"Now that you mention it, Wizly didn't have a kitchen in her house."

She probably got her nutrients from the earth around her. At that point, we probably didn't even need to call it "eating."

"But eating dirt and weeds makes my sister sad, so I want to feed her," Shalsha said, placing a salad on top of slime-Falfa.

As I watched the interaction overflowing with sisterly love (?), Beelzebub flew into the dining room, flapping her wings like she couldn't contain herself.

"We found Fighsly!"

"Yay! We've practically solved the problem!"

"Yes!"

I jumped forward, too, and Beelzebub and I shared a high five.

All we had to do next was ask this Fighter Slime.

"Fighsly was spotted in a town in the south called Kerney."

"Let's hurry and meet Fighsly!"

"We'll have Laika fly us there!"

But then Beelzebub's expression clouded.

"Well...I told it about our situation ahead of time...but it said it didn't want anything to do with worldly affairs. Apparently, it seeks nothing but strength. It said it's not a physical therapist, so it can't help us..."

Wait, wait, hold on. We're already grasping at straws here, so we aren't going to just immediately back off after that.

"If he's in a town hating those 'worldly affairs,' doesn't that just mean he's being influenced by the world anyway? I don't see why this isn't okay."

"Incidentally, Fighsly is in Kerney to participate in a martial arts tournament."

"A tournament!"

I could feel a flame erupt in my chest.

When I was a kid, I often read fighting manga that had big martial arts tournaments in them. I read girls' manga, too, of course.

"Is the tournament still accepting participants?"

"Are you going to join…?"

I nodded right away, just as Beelzebub was finishing her question.

"So if I show Fighsly that I'm stronger than him, I think he might listen to us. If I join the tournament, then we're both martial artists, right?"

Of course, he was the one making the final judgment, but we should at least get the chance to talk.

Actually, I didn't really know why Beelzebub was so hesitant.

"If you are victorious, then your name will be known in parts of the world that've never heard of you before… You'll be pulled away from your peaceful life…"

"…Oh, right…"

That was also true…

But it would be odd to send in a substitute for a mission meant to help my own daughter, so I had no choice.

"I'll do it! To bring Falfa back to normal!"

Falfa hopped up and down.

I was sure it meant something like, *I'm rooting for you, Mommy!* That was how I interpreted it.

"I see. Then I suppose I'll join as well."

"I think everyone will start panicking that the demons have come if you enter, Beelzebub…"

"It's fine. I'll join as a mystery fighter."

$$\diamondsuit$$

And so Beelzebub and I ventured to the town of Kerney and went through the process of applying. The tournament had opened three days prior, but they were pretty lenient about letting us in.

"Be careful when you fill out the form. I hear more than ten percent of applicants are disqualified because their form completion is unsatisfactory."

"That sure is a lot of people who don't fill it out properly…"

Additionally, the prize money was three hundred million gold. That was a lot.

But then something came to me.

"Wait, could the Fighter Slime have entered the tournament with the money in mind...? Does it really just want to test its strength...?"

"I can't say that's impossible. There aren't many ways martial artists can earn money anyway."

That was true—a martial artist couldn't earn money by perfecting their moves. At that point, it felt like they would become more and more like a merchant.

The day of the preliminaries came.

It would've been awful if it rained, but luckily, it was sunny.

The venue was like a coliseum. There were two stages, since there were so many matches, and each one took up its own block.

The place looked like it could fit tons of people, but it was practically empty. Unsurprising, given this was the preliminaries.

In sumo terms, it was the same kind of crowd you'd expect for the third-lowest division.

First, in the prelims, they would narrow the contest down to the best sixteen out of almost three hundred participants.

My goal today was to win until I was one of those sixteen.

I already knew this would be the case, but there were a lot of men in the waiting room. There were very few women. I still looked only seventeen years old, so people were really staring at me.

It was making me very uncomfortable, so I talked to Beelzebub about it.

"I can feel all their eyes on me, too... Men are terribly straightforward creatures..."

So Beelzebub felt the same.

She also wore a hat to hide her horns and used magic to hide her wings. This was how she was tricking everyone into believing she wasn't a demon. There was no background check, either, so that was probably doing her well.

"And what name did you enter with?"

"Beelz."

"That's it?"

"Well, the preliminaries are all just small fries, right? I just need to beat them up however I see fit. We only need to be careful not to forget the prohibition against magic. It'd be stupid if we were disqualified for that."

It was a martial arts tournament, after all, so the use of both magic and weapons wasn't allowed. We had to fight with our own bodies.

As we chatted leisurely, it soon came to my turn.

My opponent was a huge guy, way over six feet tall. His bald head glinted in the light.

"This is no place for a young lady, you know. I don't wanna end up hurting you, so I want you to withdraw."

He was something of a gentleman, it seemed. My impression of him got a bit better. At the very least, he wasn't just some dude who would come at me flailing.

"I had no intention of participating, but I have to so that my daughter can once again frolic in the hills and fields."

"Your daughter...? You already have a daughter old enough to frolic in the fields...?"

Oh no, he's got the wrong idea...

"No, I shouldn't input my personal feelings. I have to win this tournament, no matter what. If I don't—"

"Ah! Please don't tell me your personal stories, otherwise it'll be harder to defeat you!"

I would hate to hear he needed three hundred million gold in surgery fees to save his daughter!

"You're right. First, I'll defeat you to start this tournament off on the right foot!"

The bald man drew closer, so I countered with an uppercut.

That one attack knocked him right out, and he crumpled over. Well, he was still twitching, so at least he wasn't dead.

I'd never really hit people before, so I wasn't sure how much strength I needed. Still, that seemed to be good enough.

There weren't many spectators, either, so no feverish cheering followed. Great! Hopefully they'd stay this quiet.

I returned to the waiting room, and Beelz (registered name) had her arms folded, a confident expression on her face.

"You used your small physique to your advantage and got close to him quickly, then struck with an upward blow. That was the ideal attack."

"I wasn't thinking about that at all, though... I don't even have any martial arts experience..."

All it felt like was brushing off a spark that happened to fall on me.

"I see... I joined as well because I thought this would be a great opportunity to see how you fight again, but I think the reason you are so strong is because you lack a defined style..."

I felt bad for all the analysis she was doing, because I was pretty sure it was just because of my high stats.

This was the result of gradually killing slimes. It was the very essence of *slow and steady wins the race*.

After that, both Beelz and I steadily made our way up from block to block and managed to reach the top sixteen.

We were given the real tournament bracket, and I saw that Fighsly was still there. I guess there was no room for doubt—he was an incredibly powerful fighter.

We were on opposite blocks, so if we were to meet in battle, it would be at the finals.

If I did well here, then Fighsly would have no choice but to acknowledge me. Then I was confident he would cure Falfa!

◇

The family came to cheer me on at the actual tournament.

We had some of the good seats meant for family members set aside for us, so Shalsha sat with Falfa in her arms. I could spot her even from afar because she was the one with a slime.

"Do your best, Mom." Shalsha's gaze was sincere.

"Of course I will. I won't lose." I could not drop out of the tournament until I came face-to-face with Fighsly.

The event took place inside a packed coliseum.

My first battle was once again with a bald man. His muscles bulged.

"I have tempered this body of steel to repel anything and everything!!!"

I knocked away that body of steel with a swipe of my hand. "Ha!!"

My opponent lost consciousness, and victory was mine. Guess I didn't fall under *anything and everything.*

It was a one-hit KO, so the crowd went insane. It wasn't just the preliminaries anymore, so I guess that was par for the course.

"This Azusa chick is amazing!"

"She jabbed him right in the weak spot!"

"Win your next fight, please! I bet thirty thousand gold on you!"

People are already betting on me...?

I guess I couldn't tell them to stop looking at me at this point, so I accepted my spotlight and waved to the crowd.

Then I approached the family seats.

Laika and Flatorte had taken each other's hands to celebrate, but when they realized what they were doing, they immediately let go.

"I am in no mood to be friendly with a red dragon!"

"Neither am I. You have too many problems!"

So close! The excitement of victory was their chance to become friends!

As a ghost, Rosalie roamed to the waiting room and other places as she pleased.

It probably wasn't allowed, but I doubted there were any rules specifically pertaining to ghosts. No harm, no foul. At the moment, she was floating right behind Shalsha.

Sitting beside Flatorte was Halkara, who flailed an arm at me.

"Madam Teacher, I placed an advertisement for my company's drink in the coliseum! That will give me plenty of publicity!"

Now that she mentioned it, I did spot a sign that said, NEED A HEALTHY DRINK? TRY HALKARA PHARMACEUTICALS! on the wall. Halkara was really passionate about her business…

But the one most excited was Falfa. She bounded around in Shalsha's arms, like she was trying to escape, which made Shalsha look like she was bouncing on a trampoline.

"She's really happy…"

"It's given me courage and motivation as well. I'll win for sure next time. If I do, then I'll be in the top four."

Yes—glory was closer than I thought.

In my next battle, my opponent was, once again, a bald man. Was it in vogue now…?

"A hairless head is the sign of a warrior of the Grand Style! I have perfected my skills at my hometown monastery!"

I guess it was something like *Shorinji Kempo*, a Japanese martial art inspired by Shaolin kung fu.

"I will win this tournament and be the first victor from the Grand Style school in fifty-four years!"

He sure was an enthusiastic fellow…

"You may be a woman, but I won't hold back! Defeat the weak first to control the battlefield—that is the ironclad rule of Grand Style!"

"Your strategy is trash!"

What a despicable way to do things!

"Now I'll bind my opponent and deal the finishing blow!"

He grabbed my arm. I guess he was serious about that finishing blow. So I tore away from him.

"Wha—?! You broke out of my grip?! But I was told its bite was inescapable, like a snapping turtle's!"

Huh, so there were snapping turtles in this world. I'd like to eat one in a hot pot sometime.

The fight wouldn't end if I just kept evading the enemy's attacks, so I gave a roundhouse kick in my own style. If possible, I didn't want my skirt to fly up too high.

Wham!

My opponent flew thirty feet in the air, then plunged back down to the ground.

"Hmm, well, I guess that's that."

My opponent was knocked unconscious, so I got to move up to the next round, the semifinals.

If I won the next one, then I'd come face-to-face with Fighsly.

But now that I thought about it, what sort of person *was* Fighsly? Hopefully not another big bald guy. All the waiting rooms were separate during the actual tournament, so I hadn't seen what he looked like.

In the match right after mine, Fighsly's name was called.

At the same time, people started chanting, "The Prize Money Queen!"

Hmm? That wasn't the kind of response I was expecting for an aloof warrior...

Then, the person who came up on the stage had a martial artist's air, long hair tied back, and a somewhat skimpy outfit. And was a girl.

Her shoulders and belly button were showing—she was wearing a tank top, essentially. She also wore something that looked like shorts.

And in the other corner, her opponent was...Beelz, who'd won her way to this spot.

Wait, don't tell me...

In the split second right after the fight began, Beelz dealt a flurry of kicks and punches. Fighsly went right down after all that.

The judge announced the end of the match, and Beelz raised her hands in the air.

"She went down before the match even started?!"

Oh no—what to do?!

If she dropped before our face-off, then it would be much harder to get into contact with her later…

"Ha-ha-ha! With my power, wandering warriors are nothing to be feared!"

Hey! Why are you announcing your victory so proudly like that?! Aren't you forgetting the whole point of this?!

"Now, citizens, praise me! Call me the Lord of the Flies!"

And don't say things that'll give you away!

"Oh yeah, the Lord of the Flies is Beelzebub, isn't it?" "Maybe that's where the name Beelz comes from!" "That name she gave herself sure makes her a heel, huh?"

Phew. Looks like she's still in the clear. If word got out that a high-ranking demon was here, then the tournament would probably grind to a halt.

"Man, I like it when it's girl versus girl." "Yeah, all the guys are big bald dudes."

Looks like the crowd noticed, too.

Fighsly sat up and weakly staggered her way back to the waiting room. She was probably in shock after being beaten to a pulp by a dark horse.

This was bad. If she left, we'd lose our chance to talk to her.

"That Fighsly girl was nothing!"

But before I could do that, Beelzebub stepped off the stage and talked to me.

"Showing off your strength wasn't the point of this…," I said.

"Don't worry—I still have my mission to return Falfa to normal. I'll keep Fighsly from leaving, so you fight your way to the finals."

I see. Beelzebub did have time, since she'd just won, after all.

"Honestly? I don't care about the finals anymore."

My goal wasn't the money or the glory. It'd be a nuisance if people started coming to my house in the highlands for a spar.

"We will face off against each other in the finals. I am not running away. It's been quite a while, and we still have a score to settle."

I could tell right away that she was serious.

"I will absolutely find a way to save Falfa, so you must make it to the finals at all cost."

Now that she mentioned it, I realized we had never had a proper competition to settle our score.

In my last face-off with Beelzebub, she'd gotten injured when she slammed into the barrier I put up around us, and that was the end of that.

In short, it was an accident.

It was a match that really left a bad taste in my mouth. Heck, Beelzebub was down for the count before the match even began.

From that point onward, she would mention a rematch at every chance she got, but over time we also grew closer, so there really was never a good opportunity for it.

"*Sigh…* Fine, but you absolutely have to solve Falfa's problem."

"Never fear. Fighsly and I are in the same block, so her room is close to mine. I'll make sure she cooperates with us."

Beelzebub rushed off to the waiting rooms. I guess I just had to trust she would do it.

There was a bit of a break until it was time for the semifinals, so I waited, wondering if Beelzebub would bring back good news.

But that good news wasn't going to just land in my lap right away, no matter what I did.

At that point, my mind started imagining worst-case scenarios.

What would we do if even Fighsly couldn't turn Falfa back…? I was all out of good ideas…

I was still in a funk when it was my turn in the semifinals, and I joined the fight with my unease still plain on my face. I threw a punch and won.

My opponent seemed to think I was fainthearted, destined for a loss, but I wasn't so weak that a little anxiety would close the skill gap between us.

Then Beelzebub clinched her own victory and earned her ticket to the finals.

That was all fine and dandy, but I still hadn't heard anything about Falfa.

Well, Beelzebub seemed energetic enough, so that must've meant she came upon a good clue. If not, then she should've looked down, too...

This is no good. My whole brain is a mess.

Then, it was time for the finals.

I never thought my rematch with Beelzebub would take place in public.

The cheers in the arena were deafening now. No one expected it to be a fight between women.

And both of us were surprise contenders, neither the favorite for the championship, so we garnered a lot of attention.

"Witch of the Highlands!" "The rumors that she was the strongest were true!" "Beelz, the Lord of the Flies!"

I slowly stepped onto the stage.

Then, Beelzebub did the same.

It was a slow and deliberate show that stirred up the audience slightly.

"What, we finally get our big moment, and you're all cranky?"

"Of course I am. Falfa's problem hasn't been solved yet. My fight with you is a distant second on my list of priorities."

I'm not a fighting machine that thinks only of victory. I'm just a normal mom, worried about her daughter.

In fiction, you'd hear stories of baseball players promising to hit home runs for a fan's child who was combating disease, but to be frank, it didn't really matter if I won or lost.

I might as well want to win, since slime-Falfa was watching, but winning wouldn't restore her to normal.

I tried not to look over to the family seating area. I felt like that would just make my gloom worse.

"*Sigh...* Don't say things that take the excitement out of everything.

Have some appreciation for what we're doing, at least. Proclaim, *I'll avenge my previous loss!* or whatever."

It seemed that Beelzebub didn't like that I wasn't into it. I understood how she felt, but I couldn't trick myself into thinking I cared about winning.

"Sorry, but I can't take it seriously like this. If you want me to come at you with everything I have, bring me Falfa and her bright smile."

Then I'd use every skill and technique under the sun.

Beelzebub grinned. She really was starting to look like a wrestler playing the heel.

"I'll hold you to that."

"I'm sorry, but did I inadvertently commit myself to something?"

"Let me give you a surprise before we start our match."

Beelzebub turned around to face the stairs leading up to the stage and walked toward them.

There came jeers from the crowd. "Are you running away?!" "Is she surrendering the match?!"

But that wasn't it. Beelzebub was holding someone's hand.

The one following her up the stairs was—

"Mommy! Falfa's been restored!"

—my beloved daughter!

"Falfa! Falfa! Falfa! You're back to normal now!"

I immediately ran over, hugging her like a rugby player scoring a try.

Unlike when she was a slime, I could tell how warm she was.

And the way she felt in my arms was totally different, of course. I could feel her human heat, and her gelatinous texture was nowhere to be found.

"Yeah! A person named Fighsly helped me!"

Beelzebub's face said, *Gotcha!*

I see—she kept quiet so she could time the announcement…

No, wait, I think I would rather you just told me normally. You're really a lot like Pecora, you know that?

When I looked over to the family section, Halkara and the others were waving at me. They'd definitely already heard that Falfa was back to normal. I'd been totally duped. I could cheat in many other ways, but I still couldn't read people's minds.

"*Sigh*, I wish you'd told me right away, but it's not like you kept me waiting forever, so I'll forgive you."

The audience wasn't really sure what was going on, but they seemed to recognize the happy ending. I could hear a few *Awww*s.

But at the same time, I also heard, "That Azusa chick sure has a big daughter…" "I'm shocked…"

Wait, I know I look seventeen, but you're acting like I'm an idol. I can't do anything about these demands…

"Mommy, good luck! Falfa is cheering for you!"

"And now Mommy's motivation is maxed out!"

I was sure if I had an instrument that could measure power levels, it would have shattered.

"Okay, then Falfa will watch you win from a safe place."

I really didn't want to let her go, but I had to. Then, I turned my gaze to the mastermind.

"Beelzeb…*Beelz*, you'll regret showing me as much kindness as you did. Because now I can fight with more concentration than ever before."

"That's why I did this. I would hate to hear any excuses about how you were too distracted worrying about your daughter to fight."

The words of a worthy opponent.

This was going to be a serious match. Well, we couldn't use magic, so I wasn't sure if we'd be truly going at full strength, but it wasn't a bad place to do it.

After making sure Falfa was a safe distance from the stage, I took a makeshift stance.

I didn't know if the stance meant anything; I was just showing off.

I could feel the bloodthirsty waves coming off Beelzebub.

The judge signaled the start of the match.

I'll show you!

Then, Beelzebub slipped her overcoat off her shoulders. *Wait, you can't strip in front of all these people!*

Her breasts were covered, so that was a relief.

But now everyone could see her wings.

And now that her wings were free, she could no longer hide the fact that she was a demon. Sure, the rules forbade magic, but there was nothing keeping demons from participating.

"I can't fly my fastest without my wings! I never planned to fight you pretending to be someone else!"

"That's not against the rules, but the arena might panic when they see a demon. The match could be canceled, you know."

"Hell's bells, does it really matter? We completed our goal of turning Falfa back to normal, after all."

"Oh yeah, not really."

Whether the tournament was canceled or we were breaking the rules, it was all entirely trivial.

"—Then let's do this!"

Beelzebub launched herself at me with furious energy.

Whoa, whoa, a head-on fight right off the bat?! Then I'll counter!

But that said, I didn't have any fighting experience, so I wasn't exactly sure what a counter was. All I really knew was—*hit back when she comes to hit me.*

But Beelzebub skimmed the top of my head, flipping in an arc above me.

"I can't beat your speed head-on! I have to get behind you!"

"You're saying your strategy out loud!"

"That's not part of my strategy!"

I see. For me, I was just thinking to attack her when she got close. "Freestyle" was one way to call it.

It looked like Beelzebub was aiming for an opening as she spun in the air.

I'm ready when you are!

But she didn't attack me at all. Like a serious fly, she flew in circles above me.

"Shoot… This is bad…"

"You really can't find any openings?"

Could the amateur stance really have sealed the deal? Did I have some sort of hidden talent in martial arts, too?!

"You're nothing but openings… Your stance is a mess, but you're so strong for some reason… Ah, the magic of stats…"

I was so looking forward to this, but it's turning out to be a total waste of time!

"If you see the opportunity, then come at me!"

"Typically, one aims for openings because they are so rare. If you're open all the time, then it's just even harder to attack!"

What a demanding opponent.

Then I guess I should attack her— I thought about it, but she was flying.

I had magic that let me fly, but it couldn't compete with an opponent with wings that let her zip around without assistance. What I could do was float straight up in a line.

"Nothing will happen if you don't come to me, so come. Actually, you should say you're going to attack when you do. I'll be waiting."

"…I feel like you're mocking me, so I'm coming!" Beelzebub pulled her hands back, stuck her face forward, and descended at top speed.

That's one way to cut down on air resistance!

For a moment, I thought about how she would break her neck if her face-first attack landed wrong, but she probably wasn't that weak.

"I'll blow you away!"

And in response—

—I extended both my arms and waited.

When Beelzebub came, I'd catch her!

This was how you dealt with a fly!

But I definitely would not want to smack a fly with my bare hands in real life...

"Yaaah!"

And with a *clap*, I stopped Beelzebub's face with my hands.

"Abuuuuh! Don't shqueeze my fashe..."

"It's your fault for attacking face-first!"

But of course, I couldn't stop the entire force of Beelzebub's charge.

Skrrrrrrrrrrt.

I slid backward across the stage.

But after about fifteen feet, I finally stopped.

A great tremor vibrated through my body, but it didn't knock me down or render me unconscious.

"Urgh... Shtop shquishing my fashe..." Her face was contorted in a strange way.

"We're fighting, so I'll do what I want!"

"Thish ishn't an attack or anything!"

Beelzebub thrashed about, trying to get free.

I was starting to take this seriously and kept my hold on her face.

In battle, the one who fights dirtier wins. So this was probably the right answer!

"Bwah—!" Beelzebub suddenly broke free. "I never knew you'd use such an absurd defense against me... I knew such a strong amateur was bad news..."

"I'm giving you a good match! At least compliment me!"

But now Beelzebub was in point-blank range.

"I'm coming!"

I stepped forward.

Balling my fist, I aimed for her shoulder.

Even though it was a tournament, I didn't want to punch her in the face. I could probably heal it with restorative magic, but she would resist it.

Beelzebub stopped the attack with her hand.

There was a loud *wham* that echoed around us, and the arena stirred.

Not minding it at all, I threw another one.

Again, there were several great echoes.

"Shoot, just stopping you with my hand is so loud… And it hurts; it hurts so much…"

"I'm not done yet! But wow, I'm impressed you can stop my punches."

"Don't think I haven't trained for this day! I came here to win! Rain, wind, or shine, I do long training runs before and after work!"

That's the first I've heard of that!

"I wake up early and exercise for about an hour before going to work."

I guess she's a morning person.

But I hadn't expected her to do this much for our rematch. I guess she thought of us as rivals, even though it didn't seem like that at all when we saw each other.

It might be weird to say this, but I was kind of happy.

"All right! I won't lose, either!"

Beelzebub threw a series of punches and kicks at me, but I guarded with my hands and legs in my own style.

"You have great thighs," remarked Beelzebub.

"Keep the weird comments to yourself!"

"Your arms are so skinny, but you're rather tough! It's almost unfair!"

Yeah, but what can I do about it?

I could hear more cheering from the stands than I expected there to be.

"Amazing! What an exchange of technique!" "Neither one is backing down!"

To me, it felt like I was just making up the fight as I went, but it apparently looked like serious fighting moves to the spectators. Was I defending and attacking at a high speed? I wasn't aware at all.

"But you're pretty strong, Beelzebub, to go toe to toe with me!"

"Of course I am! I'm a high-ranking demon! Why wouldn't I be strong? It's far stranger that a human can stand up to me! If it was anyone but you, I would've won a long time ago! You shouldn't be able to guard against me with just your hands and legs anyway!"

Right. She was constantly coming at me, so I was starting to lose feeling in the parts I'd been guarding with. I didn't really know any demons in the neighborhood anyway.

But boy, this was tiring...

If I fought while avoiding her face, then this battle would never end.

Hitting her shoulder and stuff wouldn't put her out of commission.

How should I end it? I at least had to knock her out somehow.

But it didn't seem this fight would last forever.

Beelzebub's breath was starting to grow ragged.

"*Pant, pant...* Your guard is so tight... I'm using all I have, you know! I'm not going easy on you!"

I must have had more physical strength than her. I didn't feel tired at all.

"Why don't we just call this my victory right now?"

"I will not allow it! There's no time-out rule or anything!"

Of course she'd say that.

But we couldn't keep going forever. We had to find a way to settle who the stronger one was, but I didn't know how to do that.

Then what about a judo technique? Nah. The only move I knew was *osotogari*... I'd study more groundwork techniques next time.

For now, it didn't seem like I would lose, so I decided to strengthen my defenses.

If it came down to punching her in the face, then maybe I could go for her legs. I would just wait for an opportunity to make her give up.

—But that was the moment I heard the best call from the stands.

"Mommy! You can do it! Don't lose!"

Falfa had her hands raised above her head, waving at me as she cheered.

"Where there's a will, there's a way, Mom. Where there's a will, there's a way."

Shalsha's cheer was a little lackluster…

But it gave me energy.

Everyone else in the family was praying for my victory.

Even Flatorte was cheering at the top of her lungs. "You have to win!"

"I watched Mommy run around to help me the whole time I was a slime! I was so happy! So I'm gonna cheer as hard as I can in return!"

I was in the middle of a fight, so I couldn't respond, but— *Thank you, truly.*

Sometimes too much cheering could create a lot of pressure instead, but that didn't happen to me. It all became my strength.

"I'm sorry, Beelzebub. Now that my daughters are cheering for me, I have to show them my cool side."

"Wh-wha…?"

My body was brimming with energy.

"I've now evolved into my second form!"

"What nonsense are you talking about?! You haven't transformed at all!"

Well, of course. I'm not going to sprout horns or anything.

"Here comes a punch!" Beelzebub was growing hasty. She probably hadn't expected all of her attacks to fail.

Seizing the opportunity, I stepped forward.

Time for the counter!

Beelzebub must have been more on guard at first, but her defenses grew more haphazard over the course of the battle.

First, I just barely dodged her fist.

At the same time, I shifted my weight forward.

For a moment, I paid no mind to my own defense and concentrated only on my offense!

But I didn't punch with my fist. I spread out my right hand just below Beelzebub's face and used my palm to send a shock straight to her brain.

"Take *that*!"

I think that's called a palm heel strike.

My right hand slammed into her chin.

Her face shuddered.

And just like that, she collapsed onto the ground.

That drew the loudest cheer of the day. It almost felt like an earthquake.

"How about that? I heard that move can cause a concussion and knock people unconscious," I called out to the collapsed Beelzebub.

Knockdowns didn't factor into the rules, but I took the first down anyway.

"I'm pretty sure we can call this my win already, okay? Or can you not stand for a bit?"

Beelzebub still hadn't responded when the judge came over to check on her.

"Beelz is incapacitated. The winner is Azusa!"

Along with the call, cheers of "*Azusaaa!*" and "*She's so strooong!*" enveloped the stadium.

I did good work. I didn't mind embarrassing myself in front of total strangers, but I couldn't lose in front of my daughters. Of course, that didn't mean everything was over and done with.

Beelzebub still hadn't gotten up.

"Hey, Beelzebub, are you okay? No, you're not okay, and that's why you're on the ground…"

She still lay on her back, unmoving. She couldn't be dead, could she…?

It really had been a long time since I was in a serious fight, and since I didn't need to use all of my power, I had no idea of the limits of my own strength. I didn't think it was enough to give her a life-threatening injury…

I lightly shook her.

"Heeey, it's over. You can get up now. You should be sleeping in your bed not on the ground. Hello…?"

No response.

A chill ran through me.

I couldn't have killed her. Even though Falfa was back to normal, I couldn't be happy about it like this.

"Hey! You know the saying *all's well that ends well*? This is the opposite! We can't have it all end on an unlucky note, for multiple reasons! Understand?! Come on! Open your eyes!"

"Er, Azusa, you shouldn't shake her too much. I'll have a stretcher prepared right away," the judge called out to me from behind. I guess it would just make things worse.

"Hey, come on, get up..."

In the old romances of long past, my tears would have revived her, but I was more panicked than sad.

Well, if water would have sufficed, then there was a way.

I cast a bit of Frost magic onto her face.

That might be a good enough substitute. In terms of power, it was even better than water.

Casting it directly onto her face might make it an attack, so I cast it on the ground to make ice, then snapped off a piece of it and stuck it on her face.

"Here ya go; this'll cool you off! It'll cool you right off!"

And after ten seconds—

"B-brrrr! That's cold!"

Beelzebub woke up!

"Oh, good morning, Beelzebub!"

"That was too much! I had a dream Her Majesty the demon king froze me in ice!"

"What else was I supposed to do? Nothing else was waking you up. But I'm so relieved!"

I lifted Beelzebub up, bridal-style. She might faint again if she tried to walk, so I decided to carry her to her waiting room at least.

"Hey... This will really attract attention... And there's a big audience, too..."

"You're injured, so no complaining. You'll stumble around if you try to walk after getting a concussion like that. I saw that when I was watching martial arts on TV."

"TV? There you go with those made-up words again..."

"Oh, don't worry about that."

I nimbly carried Beelzebub off the stage. It was times like these that high stats really helped.

"I can't believe I lost to you again. It was a total defeat." Beelzebub looked invigorated.

"If you want to give it another shot, we can have a rematch sometime soon. It's a pain, though, so I don't want to."

"You're so strong, but you have no desire for blood."

That's because I didn't get stronger for the sake of strength.

"It's my way. It's just what I do. I take things little by little and enjoy life as it comes."

"I wonder if I would get stronger if I lived like that, too."

"Why not just kill slimes and only slimes?"

"Hmm… There aren't any aggressive slimes around my workplace to begin with…"

I see… She must have felt bad going out of her way to kill slimes, since they weren't attacking her first.

"But your peace may crumble again with this."

"Hmm? What do you mean?"

Don't just go and jinx me like that!

"Now word of your strength has spread to the southern part of the kingdom."

"Uh-oh…"

The entire stadium was facing me with applause.

It's an honor, but I sure hope they forget about me tomorrow!

◇

Afterward, Beelzebub and I received our award money and medals and whatnot at the award ceremony.

"The strongest witch!" "The Witch of the Highlands!" "You earned me over a million gold! Thanks!"

I waved my hand slightly in response. *I do not accept consultations that will cause trouble for me, so please don't.*

And by the way, Fighsly was at the ceremony, too. She was also receiving money, since she'd reached the higher ranks.

"Thank you so much for curing my daughter!" I bowed my head deeply. Without her, Falfa might have been stuck as a slime forever.

"I thank you, too—I was glad to have helped my own kin. It is unfortunate that my loss along the way prevented me from winning a lot of money, though." Fighsly spoke with the bright smile of an athletic girl. There was nothing slime-y about her looks.

"But I will earn more money! Even if it is just one more gold!"

"Er, um, yeah. Good luck with your earnings. Money is important."

"And if there is anything you want to know or any trouble you're having with slimes, please let me know. And please tell me if you encounter any fighting events where I might be able to earn some money."

"I thought you were supposed to be an aloof fighter, but you're pretty obsessed with money."

"My apologies, but I do have my reasons."

I wonder if she'll say it's for medical bills for her sick sister...

"Saving money is a hobby of mine."

That's so shallow!!!

Fighsly seemed a bit hesitant when she told me. It was the most worldly of worldly affairs.

"But Beelzebub told me that you didn't ask for a single coin when you cured Falfa. You're a good person, after all."

Even if she'd charged a hundred million gold, I still would have paid.

"Because we are both people in need. And...I do have something to ask of you..."

Fighsly's eyes widened as she looked up to me.

That's when I first noticed that she was rather on the short side among girls.

"And what might that be...?"

To be honest, I couldn't tell what she wanted. If she wanted money, then all she had to do was request payment for the treatment to begin with.

Because of everything that happened in the past, I did have a good amount in savings—the factory Halkara ran also played a big role in that—so I could pay what she needed of me, even if it was something ludicrous like a billion. In that case, I would end up taking a loan from Halkara, though.

Then, Fighsly bowed to an exact ninety-degree angle.

"Please, Miss Azusa! Let me be your pupil!"

"What?! Pupil, as in, a martial arts pupil, right…?"

Fighsly spoke, still bent at ninety degrees. "Yes! I have never seen anyone perform a series of such wonderful moves before! I seek the strongest fighting techniques; please allow me to study under you so that I may perfect them!"

"You know I don't have any fighting experience, right?! I'm serious when I say I don't have anything to teach you!"

Fighsly quickly stood up straight, this time at attention. Every limb down to her fingers was straight and tense.

"That can't be true. Your forms are unique. I have never seen them before!"

"Like what? I'm genuinely curious."

"Though at a glance it seems like you are full of openings, Beelz couldn't even find an opportunity to attack you in the finals. It was my first time seeing such a peculiar form. I'm certain it's because you have never allowed it to be seen by the public, yes?"

*I actually was full of openings.

"You seem completely vulnerable to attack, yet present no opportunity. This *must* be the ultimate fighting skill. The natural posture truly makes you the strongest—it's very deep! It isn't just me; anyone who continues to hone their skills would deem it something to strive for!"

Fighsly's eyes glistened.

What to do…?

I don't think she'd believe me if I told her it was just because I had high stats…

That was all I had to say, though…

"Beelz also has incredible power. It was almost like a high-ranking demon had come right to the stage. At first I thought about asking her to take me in as her pupil. But even Beelz was rendered completely helpless! You are a goddess, Azusa!"

*A high-ranking demon actually was here.

"Erm, I think you would be fine studying under Beelz…"

My strategy was to put everything on her desk.

"See, well, if I'm going to be anyone's pupil, it has to be the strongest one's!"

She's just a fangirl!

"Please! Please allow me to be your pupil! Please let me call you master!"

Oh, there she goes again with the ninety-degree bow…

"I will try my best to endure the most severe training!"

"I'm not doing any severe training at all…"

How was I supposed to make her believe me?

"Erm, I'm not saying this out of spite. I really only became strong leading a slow, lazy life. That's why I looked like I was full of openings, because I don't know any of the fundamentals. Not a single word of this is a lie!"

"…I understand."

Finally. She gets it now.

"Then please allow me one battle! Then I may truly feel for myself how powerful you are, so I may think about it on my own later!"

"You didn't understand a thing!"

Why did I end up having to fight the person I owed for the huge debt of curing Falfa?

©Benio

Life was much too short to spend punching and kicking. Wouldn't I just bring suffering on myself?

But if that would make her give up, then so be it.

We decided to fight in the corner of the arena, now that most of the audience had left.

It didn't seem like there'd be any problem if we had one little match here.

"All right, let's do this, then. But just don't start worshipping me or get disappointed because I'm not what you thought I was, okay? I haven't been bragging or anything, you know."

"Yes! Let us begin!"

She was supposedly weaker than Beelzebub, so I would just take this easy.

Fighsly immediately took her stance.

Just what I'd expected to see from someone who trained their whole life in martial arts—her posture was perfect.

Her stance and the air about her were different from people who just got in petty fights. I could tell from her aura that she was a pro.

"These skills have earned me plenty of money, you know. I'm not that weak, either."

I see. It was just as she said.

Without much of a choice, I made up my own stance in my own style.

"Yes, it is indeed an amateurish stance... So full of openings... Rather, it is *all* openings, and now I'm not so sure what is and isn't an opening..."

"You're making fun of me, aren't you?!"

But she was so serious when it came to her own stance, so it was probably inevitable that she made fun of me.

"I fought my hardest among my slime peers in order to become the unbeatable slime. And before I knew it, I was winning in battles against level-twenty adventurers."

"Poor adventurers!"

"From then on, I continued my training, and at some point, I was able to take the form of a human. After that, I spent every day training earnestly in the martial arts."

I see; she had been living with a truth-seeking mentality.

"There, I learned the importance of money in the human livelihood, and collecting money became my way of life entirely. One cannot live without money. Those without money are trash. Money can even buy love!"

"That's just twisted!"

She might've ended up with an extreme view because she was born into a world where money wasn't necessary. Poor thing…

"I'll fix that attitude of yours!"

"Then here I come! Feel the Fighsly-style slime fist!"

All right, I'll counter her like I did with Beelzebub!

She was closing the distance!

But on her way, Fighsly stopped in her tracks. Was she having a hard time attacking me *because* I had so many openings, like Beelzebub did?

But upon a much closer inspection, I saw Fighsly's legs shaking.

I heard samurai used to tremble in excitement like this, but I didn't think there would be any samurai in this fantasy world.

Wait, she was going pale, too. Was she not feeling well? I saw on the news once that a sumo wrestler suddenly got diarrhea during a match. It was awful.

"I—I'm…s-scared…"

Even Fighsly's voice was shaking.

She's scared?

Well, a regular person would probably be afraid of facing the tournament champion in battle, but she had been a participant, too, and she was the one who challenged me.

It was pretty contradictory, so I wasn't sure what she meant.

"I feel an overpowering thirst for blood looming over me like a mountain… So this is the strongest warrior…"

"Thirst for blood? I'm not like a hit man or assassin or anything…"

I'm literally just a witch taking it lazy and slow. I haven't spilled a drop of blood in my life.

"No, the aura about you is of one who has taken an unimaginable number of lives… If I draw too close… I'm going to die…!"

"Now you're just making things up! Don't talk about an innocent witch like a serial killer!"

…Hang on a sec.

I wasn't a people killer…

…But I *was* a slime killer.

And my opponent had originally been a slime.

"My slime spirit urges me to stay away from you if I value my life!"

I solved the mystery.

I was the natural enemy of slimes. People didn't usually spend three hundred years killing slimes, so there was a very high possibility that I had killed the most slimes out of anyone in existence.

It seemed Fighsly had sensed that very quickly. I guess one of the reasons she could fight so well was because her senses were so sharp.

I took a step forward.

Sweat was dripping down Fighsly's cheek.

Even though our battle hadn't truly started yet, she was in a cold sweat.

I took another step forward.

Fighsly started to lean back slightly. Her instincts were telling her to run from me.

I rushed right up to her.

"D-don't kill me…"

Fighsly collapsed on the spot, her eyes still open.

It looked like her fear made her give up trying to comprehend me.

"A true warrior strikes her opponent down without even touching her… Pfft, yeah, right."

I won, but only because I'd become some kind of indefinable monster to her. As a girl, I fell into a very complicated frame of mind.

Boy, was that rude…

Thirty minutes later, Fighsly woke up.

"Huh? This is…my dressing room…"

"Yes, I carried you here for the time being."

"—Wah! If it isn't Azusa, the strongest creature on the planet!"

Sheesh, I might have to report this to someone as harassment soon…

"I didn't think it would end before we even made contact. I don't think you gained anything from it, but I'm not taking responsibility for that, okay?"

"Yes… I still lack training. I have learned that I cannot even draw close to something so terrifying. I must temper myself even more."

Okay, but treat me like a woman. Or at least like a human!

I only look seventeen years old, okay?! If I were still in Japan, people would see me as a high school girl!

"Oh! Miss Fighsly is awake!" There came an adorable voice from behind me. It was Falfa, and with her were the other members of the family. And Beelzebub. "You've been waiting all this time alone, so I called everyone here!"

"The match is already over. I'm leaving," Beelzebub said.

Fighsly looked to Beelzebub, and the color in her eyes changed.

It was, without a doubt, a gaze of admiration.

"Aaah! It's Beelz! Thank you for such a spectacular tournament! I will work my hardest and earn more money than you next time!"

Can this girl not get through a conversation without mentioning money?

"It's thanks to you that Falfa is back to normal. We should be thanking you," Beelzebub said generously.

"Thank you again, Miss Fighsly! Falfa's got her body back now!"

The polite Falfa gave her thanks with a smile. *Good girl—she said a proper thank-you. My teachings are very thorough!*

"Oh, no. This was nothing special. But your mother is an extraordinary person, Falfa."

"Yeah! Mommy's the strongest in the world!"

Her excitement and wording were just like a regular child declaring their mommy was the nicest in the world, but in my case, it was very possible that I was actually the strongest person in the world. I wasn't particularly proud of that, though.

"I see your words are pure and truthful. I must hone my skills even further..."

I was glad to see she had aspirations. I hoped she wouldn't die during her training, just in case either Falfa or Shalsha turned into slimes again.

"And so, Lady Beelz, would you accept me as your pupil?" Fighsly bowed her head before Beelzebub.

"What? Why must I do such a thing?! I have no intentions of taking in pupils!"

Beelzebub lightly brushed her away. It did seem like a big pain, after all.

"In this tournament, I have learned of demon-like strength! Please allow me to train under you!"

"Indeed. Those like demons are never surpassed. Yet they don't take pupils. Should I put my all into training them, I may find myself beaten to a pulp by my own underlings."

"What? Your day job is something completely different, yet you're that strong?! When do you train?"

Thinking about it normally, that was surprising.

"I train a bit when I can. Though I neglected it up until I met Azusa. I've been training in order to even the score, but it hasn't been enough."

"Please! Please take me as your pupil!"

"Not my problem! I'm not one to be teaching others anyway!"

I was surprised to see how firmly Beelzebub was refusing. Her instinct must have determined that this girl was a nuisance.

"Aw, you should take her on as your pupil." (Meaning, if we kept track of where she was, it'd help if either of my daughters turned to slimes again.)

"Your ulterior motives are *way* too obvious!"

"Please! I will wash dishes! I will do anything!"

As I watched the exchange, I gave Falfa a hug.

"Falfa, you can ask for anything you want today, okay? Is there anything you want to eat?"

"Mommy, Falfa wants to eat candy!"

Eventually, Beelzebub allowed Fighsly to be her pupil after much pestering.

I was excited to find out what Fighsly's reaction would be when she went to Beelzebub's home.

But a slime was a monster, so she would probably be fine.

FALFA AND SHALSHA

Spirit sisters born from a conglomeration of slime souls. Falfa, the older sister, is a carefree girl who's honest about her own feelings. Shalsha, the younger sister, is considerate and attentive to others. They both love their mother, Azusa.

HALKARA

A young elf woman and Azusa's second apprentice. Everyone in the family (particularly Azusa) admires her periodic bouts of maturity and her enviably perfect looks… That doesn't change her role as the family member with a knack for screwing up.

BEELZEBUB

A high-ranking demon known as the Lord of the Flies. She frequently shuttles between the demon realm and the house in the highlands, both to get the Nutri-Spirits Halkara makes and to dote on Falfa and Shalsha as if they were her nieces. She's Azusa's reliable "big sister" surrogate.

Falfa was back to normal, and peace had returned to the house in the highlands for the first time in a while.

"All right, today will be my special salad. Please drizzle on some sesame dressing before eating it!"

Everyone energetically dug in to the vegetable salad Halkara made for breakfast.

Not counting my two daughters, who had been alive for only about fifty years, everyone in my family had ages in the triple digits. We were a long-lived family, but we also paid close attention to our health.

"Hmm… Vegetables are good for looks, but I do want to have a good portion of meat sometimes."

"That's where I agree with you, Laika."

Both Laika and Flatorte were sounding very much like dragons.

"Sure, I can see how this wouldn't fill up a dragon."

"That's correct, mistress. We dragons are what we are because we devour meat. This will just make me too skinny."

It must've been especially draining for Flatorte, who was typically a bigger eater than Laika.

"Um, it kind of sounds like you're dissing my salad, and that makes me sad…"

Halkara looked a little glum. Halkara was an elf, and the vegetarian lifestyle was normal for her, so of course any complaints about that would make her upset.

On the other hand, Rosalie was observing us from the ceiling, nodding in great interest as though we were mere objects of study.

"There sure is a lot for the living to think about when it comes to eating."

She probably felt like someone who had no interest in fishing at all side-eyeing a bunch of excited anglers.

"Anyway, salad is a meal on its own, so please eat it. If you want meat, then when it's my turn, I'll be sure to purchase some chicken. There is a shop in Nascúte that sells very delicious chicken."

Halkara ran a factory in Nascúte, so she was an expert on the shops there.

"No, Halkara, that's not it. Chicken is—how to put this—weak." The expression on Flatorte's face read, *She doesn't get it.*

"About that… I sort of understand how she feels."

Laika's expression was muted, which basically meant that she agreed with Flatorte.

They were contending with each other, but their thoughts were often on the same page. There were probably many subtleties I wouldn't understand unless I was a dragon.

"Basically, chicken is a bird, of course. I don't feel full after eating bird. See, it's much too light. I may as well eat a giant omelet—that would be much better."

"I understand that, but the only creatures we could hunt in the land where I'm from were birds, or deer at the most."

"Aah, deer. That doesn't quite hit the spot, either. Anyway, unless it's meat from something that's more of a *beast*, I don't really feel like I've eaten my fill. Maybe not so much 'eaten my fill' but more like, I don't feel truly *alive*. Vegetable salad is much too well mannered. Shouldn't we devote ourselves to the joy of eating?"

"I've started to understand what Flatorte's talking about."

This was like when a bunch of high school boys headed for an all-you-can-eat *yakiniku* barbecue shop once club activities were done for the day.

Well, high school girls, too. Athletes ate a *lot*.

"To be frank with you, eating too much meat is bad for your health. It's a problem of nutritional balance. Not only that, but forcing yourself to eat until you're completely stuffed is even worse. But"—I lightly hit the table—"life sometimes calls for a food and drink binge. Animals have urges to act uncivilized!"

I recalled a memory I had of stuffing my face full at an all-you-can-eat *yakiniku* buffet.

That wasn't too bad.

"Yes, mistress! You understand the feelings of dragons well!"

Flatorte complimented me. I didn't really understand how dragons felt, only how high schoolers felt. And thus was born my theory: High school student athletes were dragons.

"Falfa likes meat, too!"

Falfa energetically raised her hand, and Shalsha sat nodding beside her. Maybe it was because my two daughters were slime spirits, but they were happy to eat anything. They did like meat better than vegetables because they were kids, though.

"But game meat is difficult to procure around here. There isn't much for us to find in the wild." Laika tilted her head in thought.

She was right. The highlands around here were much too peaceful.

But of course, that was my own doing.

I had requested a leisurely life when I was being reborn, so naturally, I was reincarnated in an area with weak monsters and animals.

"We can travel on Laika and Flatorte, so we should investigate areas with lots of animals. I hope that's okay with you."

I guess that was our common ground.

But in that case, we should just make a trip out of it and find a spot to turn into our picnic ground.

Knock, knock, knock.

There was a rather gentle rapping at the door.

Judging by the sound, I was 90 percent sure it was a woman. Or maybe they were just hesitant because it was morning and we might've still been sleeping.

I opened the door, and there was Natalie.

She worked at the guild in Flatta. Our household's livelihood depended on the magic stones that came from defeating slimes, and since the guild was where I exchanged the stones for money, I knew Natalie well.

In terms of profits alone, Halkara's factory made much, much more, but as a general rule, that money went into Halkara's wallet.

"Oh, I don't often see you knocking on my door, Natalie. Are you off from work at the guild today?"

"No, I still have time before my shift, so I decided to come to you directly. It is a bit of an urgent matter."

I went in to exchange once or twice a week, so I never went longer than a week without seeing her.

"What is it? If you're coming to me, then you're probably going to ask me to defeat some monsters, right?"

I wasn't an adventurer, but if monsters started popping up in the village, I could deal with those, at least.

"They're not monsters, strictly speaking, but wild animals…"

Were they that dangerous?

"Oh, come in, come in. You're here already—I want you to tell the whole family anyway."

I welcomed Natalie into the house.

Shalsha seemed a little shocked to see a visitor for once, but we had no problems. Everyone was very well behaved.

"All right, then, Natalie, please tell us what it is."

"It isn't in this province, but two provinces over, there's a wood called Nilka Forest."

"Okay."

Shalsha heard the name and returned to her room, probably to get some kind of geographic reference.

She had a whole slew of books in her room. Books were valuable in this world, so if worse ever came to worst, that was enough to be a fortune on its own.

"There's a kind of boar that lives in Nilka Forest called the long-hammer boar."

"I feel like I've heard a name like that before... Oh, I killed a monster called the long-spear boar once."

That happened on the way to Laika's sister's wedding.

"Their names are similar, but this is an animal not a monster. They don't drop magic stones. Their head is long and durable, and they kill their prey by head-butting them."

I wasn't surprised to hear a beast like that existed.

"There's been a dramatic increase of long-hammer boars lately, and it's apparently too much for the local adventurers. Even the most skilled are having a tough time... I hear that there are so many of them that the party just gets surrounded, endangering them."

"I've heard that can be a problem when there are too many. I don't really understand, though."

From what I'd heard from adventurers, monsters that are no big deal in a one-on-one can immediately become a threat when in a mob.

Like how fifteen jobs that each take an hour to complete are no joke when you have a day to complete them.

They made me do those things like it was no big deal back when I was a corporate wage slave... There was no assumption that I'd be let home at a specific time... *No, no. Bad memories are resurfacing. Let's turn the talk back to the boars.*

"But they have an adventurers' guild, so couldn't they just send out a request for help?"

I felt bad for asking, but if they were outsourcing this kind of work, then the job probably required more bodies than we had available. You could definitely find adventurers out there who were willing to kill such creatures.

"Actually... The region around Nilka Forest has a very low

population…and there's no money at all to hire such a large number… They can pay quite a bit for a small few, but once they need ten or more heads, they really, really can't…"

They needed the numbers, but they didn't have the money to guarantee them. Must be hard living in the countryside.

At that point, I'd want the government to step in, but given this world's values, it was entirely likely they'd just be told to vacate the area and move elsewhere. I sort of understood why they wouldn't invest in such a small town.

"The increasing numbers of long-hammer boars are starting to appear around human settlements. At this rate, it might actually reach the point where they'll have to abandon the village…"

So that's why she came to me in a rush. The village would be in danger if something wasn't done soon.

"A request for help came to our guild. They said the great Witch of the Highlands and her entourage may be able to get rid of the boars in no time and with the help of only a few people…"

To be honest, this sounded like a job I could do and still be back in time for dinner.

If I could use my power to stop a village from being destroyed, then I may as well. It wasn't like it put me in much of a bind.

"Then I underst—"

"Yes, I'll do it!" Flatorte cut me off, responding enthusiastically. "I'll hunt one a minute, even more than that. I know I can manage that, even in human form."

"Flatorte, you're really into this… Well, not like it's a problem, though."

"Mistress, I know this request was tailor-made for us dragons!"

I couldn't quite parse what she meant.

"These boars aren't monsters, correct? Which means when we kill them, they won't become a magic stone but will instead leave behind a carcass."

"Yes, that is how it works."

"Which means—this'll be an all-you-can-eat boar party!"

Clack!

Now Laika inadvertently leaped to her feet.

"That's it! That way we can get an unbelievable amount!"

"My stomach can finally rejoice for the first time in so long! We *have* to go!"

This was probably the first time I'd seen the dragons so passionate…

We never had any romantic escapades in this household, and everyone really had more of an appetite for food than romance anyway…

Natalie stared at my family blankly.

"Um, you may eat them, sure… But it'll be much more than just one or two boars, you know… I hope you understand that you can't just eat two and be done with it…"

It certainly did seem like food was their only concern.

"That should go without saying. I'd eat a hundred heads, or even two hundred!"

She was counting them by *heads*, like a farmer. Did she mean literal heads or the whole thing? How much was she planning on eating?!

"Boar meat would probably taste gamey. Do you know a good way to prepare it, then?"

We would likely have to carefully extract the blood right after killing it to keep the meat from tasting weird.

"Mistress, dragons are perfectly content with gamey meat!"

"Lady Azusa, the peculiarity of the meat is what makes boar taste like boar."

They both explained fervently.

The world of dragons runs deep…

$$\diamond$$

We all rode on both Laika and Flatorte in their dragon forms and headed toward Nilka Forest.

We also had to go to the village for an account of the situation, so Natalie came along.

Natalie seemed pretty hesitant, this being her first time aboard a dragon, but she quickly got used to it and started enjoying sightseeing from the sky. She sure had guts.

Maybe working in a job that dealt with rowdy adventurers gave her that grit.

First, we alighted in the village, gave our greetings to the mayor, and pinned down where the long-hammer boars were appearing.

"There's a small river in the wood, and it seems the boars often go there for water."

"A barbecue by the riverside... That sounds lovely..."

"It's like we're camping. How rustic!"

I could almost see the drool pouring out of the two dragons' mouths.

"Then we'll be off. But...just to be safe—Falfa, Shalsha, Halkara, stay here."

Boars could be rather violent in their own way. There was still a chance the others could get hurt.

"Madam Teacher, I want to go into the forest to collect mushrooms, though..."

"I know how you feel, Halkara, but you have to be careful this time."

I felt bad, but the only outcome I saw for her was one where the boars caught her.

"Miss Halkara, I want to go to the village's museum of history and folklore."

"You've got the tastes of an old lady, don't you, Shalsha? But I guess it might be a nice way to pass the time," Halkara commented. It looked like she would act as babysitter for me, so the rest of us would go clean up some boars in the meantime.

The two dragons and I pushed into the woods, along with Rosalie the ghost acting as a scout.

Laika and Flatorte were still in their human forms. It wouldn't be much of a solution to the problem if they froze or burned up the whole forest in their dragon forms.

"Oh, I now see why the boars are reproducing as much as they are. The roads are dangerous and poorly maintained. Since it is so hard for humans to use them, the boars are multiplying safely."

Laika's impressions were probably correct.

There wasn't much of a difference between the human and animal trails in the forest. One step off the road would land us straight in the underbrush.

On top of that, the vines and spiderwebs everywhere were super annoying.

"We're fine, since we have such high-level skills, but regular adventurers would definitely hate this..."

"Meat, meat, it's almost meat time! ♪" And among it all, Flatorte was the only one weirdly enthusiastic. "Juices overflowing, bursting like a fountain. ♪ Drink it all up! ♪"

Does she seriously like meat that *much?* I wondered, but I guess her lust for meat was just an indication of how healthy she was.

When I had still been working in the office, I often heard words like *vegan* and *LOHAS*, but I didn't really understand what they were.

The impression I got was that people were turning food into fashion, and I didn't really like it...

*Just my personal opinion.

When the dragons decided to turn this into an eating contest, I was unsure about letting them essentially play with their food, but eating one's fill was an animal's instinct. It probably wouldn't be too bad.

Rosalie slipped through the trees, investigating whatever was ahead. She was essential for our plan this time.

But in a way, didn't constantly staying as a ghost make her the most unfairly overpowered of all?

"I've seen most of what's ahead. If you keep going straight, you'll go downhill and end up at a mountain stream. Stay on your current path! There are about fifteen boars at the river."

According to Rosalie's explanation, we had a good number of boars ahead.

"Fifteen boars... All right, let's do this! Bring it on!"

Flatorte's enthusiasm blazed even brighter, and she dashed through the forest.

"Please refrain from acting independently!"

"Laika, this is when you call upon your wild instincts! Don't stop me!"

Laika seemed to understand what Flatorte was saying, and she couldn't say any more.

That being said, vines and twigs were blocking the way—

By the time the ground started sloping downward, Flatorte got caught on a small branch.

"I struggled to get free, but now I'm even more trapped... It's rather elastic, so it's not snapping very easily..."

"See? This is what happens when you try to force your way forward like that..."

I disentangled Flatorte from the branch. She would doubtlessly be able to peel herself free if she changed into a dragon, but I guess that wasn't an option.

"Oooooh! It's the clothes' fault that I got caught on it!"

"And what will getting angry about it accomplish? Of course you have to wear clothes."

I sighed impatiently and freed Flatorte from the tree.

Flatorte gripped her clothes and tugged at them. It was like she was seeing them for the first time in her life.

"...Now that my wild instinct has gotten stronger, my clothes are just getting in the way," she said and started removing them on the spot.

I say *removing*, but that is too polite of a word. She was flinging them off violently, practically hurling them every which way.

"H-hey, wait a second! What are you doing?!"

"Have you lost your mind?!"

"Hmm, I see. So if you're still alive, you can take off your clothes."

Rosalie was the only one voicing an irrelevant opinion, but this was a bit of an unusual situation.

Where on earth did girls who wanted to get naked in a forest come from?!

"Mistress, I apologize. This may sound obvious, but blue dragons don't wear clothes when they're in dragon form. So clothes are nothing but a nuisance... I've been enticed by the prospect of eating boars, and I'm very tempted to return back to my regular self."

"That may be true, but this is terrible manners for a girl!"

She continued to remove her clothing as we talked, and she was now down to her underwear. She was a real problem child!

"Please don't worry. No one is here in these woods. No one knows I'm naked, so it's just the same as if I was clothed."

"What kind of metalogic is that?!"

Also, that was how you jinxed yourself. It was safer not to say those things.

Flatorte finally removed her underwear and tossed it away, and I could see exactly where her tail connected to the rest of her body.

"I'm free! I'm freeeeeee!"

Then, she dashed down the slope with so much energy, it was hard to tell if she was falling or running.

"Aaand she's off..."

"I'm sorry, Lady Azusa. I apologize on behalf of all dragons... She has always had bouts of unpredictability. One time, she felt like fighting with a red dragon, so she came to me..."

Laika put a hand to her forehead.

"I think I understand."

It didn't seem like the plan behind the attack on the wedding had been particularly elaborate, either.

"She is an idiot at heart... But she is able to get things done, and I've heard she's unified the blue dragons. Still, getting things done is all she does, and she has a hard time displaying leadership or taking definitive measures…"

"Sounds like a handful for red dragons, too…"

Well, there probably weren't any other adventurers around to take care of the boars for the reward, so she probably wouldn't run into any perverts in the woods.

But any adventurers who encountered her would sure be in for a shock… They'd probably wonder what the heck was going on with this naked girl sprinting toward them.

"The path ahead is pretty steep, so please proceed with caution."

"Thanks, Rosalie. We'll take our time."

We proceeded slowly down the path for another fifteen minutes, and then Flatorte was approaching us from ahead, crying for some reason.

"When I got to the river, there were people, and they saw me naked…"

"See? That's why I told you to wear your clothes… They didn't do anything to you, did they?"

"I think they were women, so it was okay. They seemed startled."

Actually, it was probably more of an ordeal for the witnesses.

"I've brought along your clothes. Put them on here."

Laika handed over her clothes. It was times like these that her dependable nature really shone.

"Th-thanks, Laika… I owe you…"

"You don't owe me anything. Just get yourself dressed."

Then, once Flatorte put her underwear back on—

"All right, this shouldn't be too embarrassing! Keep the rest."

"I'm sorry?"

"I'm going back to the river!" She whirled around and ran off.

Hey! Why do you think wearing just your underwear makes it okay?!

"Laika, we're going after her. They might think there's a group of crazy exhibitionists out here!"

"Indeed… Let's put clothes back on her!"

"I am a ghost, so I can go as fast as I need!"

We dashed through the trees for the river.

After a little while, we started hearing the burble of water, so we were getting close to our destination.

Five minutes later, we found the river.

It was shallow but over fifteen feet wide, so it was a reasonable watering hole for the long-hammer boars.

"Ah, the wind feels so nice!"

Flatorte was jumping around in her underwear.

"I wish you wouldn't try to convince me how nice it feels dressed like that... There were people around, weren't there...? Put on some clothes."

"They must have left. I don't see them."

She was right; it seemed like we were the only ones around.

Alternatively, the nude Flatorte scared them off...

That was the most likely possibility.

"Oh, and mistress, now is not the time for clothes."

"Clothes are a priority in most situations, actually."

"No, our enemies are approaching."

I took a look around the area, and the long-hammer boars were collecting nearby.

Their protruding heads looked incredibly tough.

Some of them were even shaking their heads, as though intimidating us. Were they just practice swings?

"I see. They're raring to attack people. Let's bring this to an end."

"Yes. Let us begin the hunt, mistress!"

"I will show you the results of my special training destroying slimes with Lady Azusa!" Laika called it "special training," but it really wasn't that special.

We all faced the closest boar to ourselves.

First, I watched to see how the animal would act.

It quickly came at me for a head-butt, and I evaded it right away.

Its movements were sharp. An adventurer might be terrified if they found themselves in a circle of these.

I deliberately stopped a head-butt with my hand once. It was a fairly heavy blow.

"I see. They're pretty powerful fighters in their own right."

The boar hadn't knocked me away, so it started to whine in panic and confusion.

Well, time to take care of this!

I punched its head.

From the feeling under my hand, one good hit was more than enough. It probably put a sizable dent into the bone or even broke it in two.

The boar staggered, then collapsed on its side. I was level 99, after all.

The next one drew closer for a hit, but I crouched down and gave it an uppercut.

The boar sailed through the air in an arc, then thudded to the ground.

My attack was made specifically for my opponent, so it was twitching even if it wasn't dead.

"Hmm, yeah, that's about right."

My attacking hand still didn't feel like resting yet, but I'd finally gotten the hang of it.

How were the other two doing?

Laika was dealing a rapid flurry of punches like a boxer, overwhelming the boars.

"A good offense is the best defense! You won't find any chance to attack me!"

At last, she dealt a clean kick to a boar that sent it flying. KO. She was defeating them swiftly and cleanly, with textbook technique.

I guess even in her human form, she wouldn't lose to enemies this weak.

Next, boars tried to head-butt her from either side, but she timed her jump perfectly so that the two ran right into each other.

"You lack training."

They didn't train. They were boars.

All right, Laika seemed fine, so how about Flator—

"W-wait! Give that back!"

She was chasing a boar that had somehow snagged her bra on its head.

"Hey! What on earth are you doing?!"

"Mistress, I was trying to evade it, but my undergarments were caught on my opponent... Hey! You can't get away! You're supposed to face me in battle!"

She was acting a little like a caveman...

And yet, Flatorte would greet any nearing boars with a firm strike. She was taking care of the problem, but she just couldn't seem to defeat the bra thief in question.

"I finally caught you!"

The boar burst under a magnificent dropkick, and it flew over to the river and plopped into the water.

And her bra was starting to drift downstream.

"Aaaaaaaah! It's floating away! I'm sorry! This is all my fault! It's because I suddenly stripped!"

Oh, how cruel...

Flatorte reached out, but the bra just widened the gap.

The situation was growing dire.

The other boars had managed to get their heads in Flatorte's other clothes where we had set them aside, and now they were running around with them.

They had been rummaging through our things, wondering if there was any food, and that was probably how they ended up like this.

"Noooooo! I'll be in so much trouble going home if I lose all my clothes! I can give up my underwear at the most, but you can't take thaaaaaat!"

Terrible desperation crossed her face.

Was she going to seriously engage with just a little boar?!

"Blue Dragon Kick!"

Flatorte's attack connected, and the boar was sent to the wind like so much paper. Then, along with her clothes, the boar dropped into the river.

Yup, along with her clothes. It was almost cliché at this point.

Flatorte's garments bobbed elegantly down the river.

"*Aaaaaaaah!* Wait, wait! I know they're not my favorites, and I was actually thinking about throwing them out after they got dirty today, but— Wait!"

Come on, Flatorte, think of where you're kicking... But at times like these, any plans she could make would just backfire on her anyway.

Flatorte stood there in a daze, and behind her appeared another long-hammer boar.

Its head caught on her underwear.

Oh...I know what's happening.

"Wait! Let's talk, okay?! For goodness' sake! For goodness' *sake*, you can do anything else, just not this! I know I was talking on and on about my instincts earlier, but dragons are civilized creatures, you know!"

Rrri, rrrrrrrrrrrip...

Her underwear passed into the past tense, transforming into scraps of fabric.

And when that happened, something switched on inside Flatorte.

"Enough... All right, you boars! Since you are without clothes, I, the magnificent Flatorte, shall face you in battle unclothed as well! I'm through playing around, okay?! Do you understand?! What's wrong with nudity? Is there any animal that's born wearing clothes? No, there isn't! There's nothing strange about me!"

Yeah... I think there is. What you're doing is definitely weird.

But she probably wasn't going to be listening anymore.

With vim and vigor, Flatorte hunted the boars.

After half an hour, we took a short break from clearing out the boars.

In the end, we defeated over a hundred of them, including the pack nearby. There were heaps of them stacked around the river.

They were considerably aggressive, so they all sought us out to attack us. Which meant the more we defeated in this battle, the more efficient it was, in a way. It would take way too much time if we were the ones pushing into the woods to fight them.

But for the two dragons, this was apparently just the beginning.

Laika immediately began setting up the barbecue equipment on the riverbank.

She brought a lot of things with her, but it looked like everything was for just that.

Once she was finished setting up, she took a big knife and concentrated on cutting away the meat. She was being somewhat careful so that the meat wouldn't start to smell, but there was just so much. She cut and cut and cut.

On the other hand, Flatorte was calmly and nakedly gathering firewood for the fuel.

"Phew, I feel so good after taking a walk around! We're roasting and eating boar in the forest! These are the true pleasures of the great outdoors!"

You're way too naked to be as enthusiastic as you are! And I'm surprised to hear the concept of "the great outdoors" exists in this world!

I really wanted to show this scenery to people in Japan who talked about "glamping" or "glamorous camping."

There was not the slightest bit of luxury in sight, and our only ingredient was boar meat.

"Rosalie, does it look like any boars will attack us soon?"

"The boars have been completely beaten back, and so it seems they've withdrawn. We should be fine for the time being. It doesn't seem like there are any other herds nearing, either."

Then it looks like we can finally begin our feast.

"This should be big enough."

Laika breathed fire to light the barbecue. It was surreal to watch fire coming out of a girl's mouth, but I was used to it by now.

The meat sizzled, and healthy white smoke drifted from the grill.

"Fat is splashing everywhere! It's hot!"

"You're totally naked, so don't be so careless! Stay away from it!"

I was mostly taking care of the meat. The other two would be completely fine eating it rare, so I was a bit apprehensive.

Really, I wasn't so weak that rare meat would make me sick, but mentally, I couldn't stand the thought. When I'd gotten food poisoning in my previous life, I was in pain for days...

"All right, here we go! Barbecue under a blue sky!"

""Oooh!""

There probably wasn't any barbecue sauce in this world, so I brought salt.

Grill, salt, eat. That was it.

It tasted very gamey, but salt was simple and strong enough to keep that in check, so it wasn't too bad.

It felt like real hunting.

"This is good! So delicious!"

"Yes! Lady Azusa, we must eat up!"

"Now this is a meal! This is what food should be like! Now we eat like barbarians!"

It's kind of convincing when she says it naked...

In the beginning, we were all eating at about the same pace, but our differences were starting to show after ten minutes.

I was getting tired of nothing but boar, but the other two were actually picking up the pace.

They were using a huge metal plate to grill, but it was continuously filled with the next serving.

Grill, eat, grill, eat.

Like a perpetual engine, over and over.

"It's so, so, so good!" Flatorte crowed.

"Yes. I feel the energy spreading throughout my entire body!" Laika agreed.

"Table manners? Human manners? Pshaw, get out of here!"

"It's not a very refined taste, but such a fun meal doesn't need to be!"

I was so impressed—dragons will be dragons.

"To eat is to live, I see, Big Sis." Rosalie drifted to my side.

"I'm sorry. I know you can't eat, but it still feels like we're showing off."

"No, it's all right. I've never seen Laika so radiant before. Thank you for the show. And since ghosts don't have an appetite, it's not that painful."

Now that she said it, I understood. She didn't need it to survive, so she never had the desire to eat.

"Why don't you possess someone and take a bite? There's a river here, too, so you can leave if you jump in. And we already have someone naked, so your clothes won't get wet."

"Then I'll give it a shot, once I have permission."

Rosalie possessed Flatorte.

And once she had, she yelped and covered herself. "I'm naked! This is so embarrassing!"

Huh, so ghosts gain a sense of shame when they're in a physical body...

Rosalie's impressions after taking a bite were, "It's a bit gamey..."

It didn't seem that she liked it very much. It probably looked and tasted the best to her before she even took a real bite.

Afterward, Rosalie jumped into the river in Flatorte's body and got out with no issues.

"My body's cooled down from the water, so time to warm it up with more food!"

She bit into the meat again, her breasts swaying.

I was becoming desensitized. I barely even noticed Flatorte was naked anymore.

Laika in turn was also gnawing on the meat. She didn't need any carbs. Just meat.

I had also had my fill and was starting to feel a little overstuffed, but just like Rosalie, I was having a fun time watching.

Then I realized why I was so pleased with the whole situation.

"I feel like I've always wanted to have a girls' day out like this..."

In my previous life, a girls' day out mostly just meant chatting in fancy restaurants.

At least, that was true in my experience.

It was comfortable, since it was only us girls. There was no need to worry about the gazes of the opposite sex. But we were still watching one another, I guess.

As we carefully chose our topics of conversation, we would offer information to paint ourselves in a flattering or impressive light, one-upping one another as we talked.

Even though we worked in different places. None of us was even fighting. And yet most of us were trying to convince the others that we were happier.

I often felt, *This feels so empty. Isn't your whole life just posting pictures of the nice food you eat to Instagram?*

But that wasn't the case here.

We were just grilling and eating boar. And one of us wasn't even wearing clothes.

Had I gone on this kind of girls' day out when I was still a corporate slave, then my stress would've gone way down. I probably would've enjoyed it.

As I reflected, Rosalie came back in a hurry from her scouting mission.

"Big Sis! Someone's coming!"

"What? Oh no, what should we do? We still have Flatorte here!"

"But it's someone we know."

Beelzebub flew in, carrying Vania.

"What on earth are you doing…?" She looked at us dubiously when she asked. Well, we were being pretty dubious ourselves, so I wouldn't argue.

"Er, grilling boar," I answered honestly.

"We came because we thought we should give these to you."

In Vania's hands were Flatorte's clothes that had washed down the river!

"I was wondering what they might be at first, but I knew whoever lost them must be upset about it, so I went searching for the owner."

"Thank you, Vania! This is a big help." I gave thanks in Flatorte's place.

Flatorte was also happy in her naked glory. "Phew! What a relief!"

"You lot truly show up everywhere."

Beelzebub seemed a bit annoyed, but we'd known each other long enough that she was used to it.

Laika turned into a dragon to spit fire and dry the clothes. The strength of her dragon form's flames was greater than her human form's. What a luxury, to use a dragon this way.

"But you sure ate a lot of boar. I'm impressed. Why don't we have a bit as well? Is that all right?"

"Yes, please, have as much as you like, actually. It all tastes the same, so I'm starting to get bored…"

I handed some leftover forks to Beelzebub and Vania.

The two demons filled their mouths with meat like it was water, betraying their appearances. Demons really did eat well…

"Mm, not bad."

"This rustic approach is quite nice, but I almost feel like making a few adjustments," Vania said, then brought out a large box. "I have my cooking set."

In the box were spices and other ingredients, as well as a pot and other cookware. It looked like she was going to start cooking straightaway.

"Huh? Do you carry that around with you?"

"Cooking is also part of my job, so I must always be in the spirit to cook, wherever and whenever."

She *had* taken care of food for us when we were on the way to the demon's castle.

"The meat is rather high-quality, and I believe I can make a lovely wild game dish from this!"

And in a very short amount of time, she produced the boar meat on a plate with a drizzle of sauce on top and herbs on the side.

"All right. I believe it will taste a bit different this time, so you will be able to eat even more."

I immediately took a bite, and it tasted like the real deal.

This is as good as something you'd order at an expensive French restaurant!

"Vania, you're practically a pro chef!"

"I am a pro chef! I've treated you before, haven't I?!"

"Yes, she has a chef's license, after all. She is much better suited for cooking than office work."

Huh, so demons can get cooking licenses.

Beelzebub sat on a large boulder, elegantly enjoying the food. She sure looked like she belonged in high society.

Both Laika and Flatorte also seemed satisfied with a professional's true skill.

By the way, since Flatorte's clothes still weren't dry, she was eating in her underwear.

I might as well think of it like a swimsuit and drop the issue.

"Of course, if we were in an environment where I could use even more ingredients, I would like to try many other things, but I think this is the best I can do for now. Please come to Vanzeld Castle again."

"Yeah, definitely."

"O-oh, okay… You're coming again… I have to…get ready…"

Beelzebub didn't seem as upset as I thought. She was actually weirdly shy about it.

"Yeah, this is delicious! This is the fate that my nudity brought us! Sometimes it's good to go naked!"

Well, she wasn't *completely* wrong, but that brand of positive thinking was a little absurd!

When we get home, I'll have to give her a good lecture on wearing clothes.

Away from the rest of us, Laika finished her meal and once again breathed fire to dry Flatorte's wet clothes.

"Hell's bells. We were here by the river when some naked lady suddenly appeared and scared the living daylights out of us… Vania even fell straight into the river…"

Oh, so it was Beelzebub and company who were originally by the river. I suppose the list of people who would come to a place like this was pretty short.

"I gather the long-hammer boars have had their ranks sufficiently thinned," Beelzebub commented.

"Formally, we're here by the guild's request. Boy, I never thought there'd be this many boars."

Suddenly, a question came to me. I should have thought of it earlier, but the whole naked incident had shocked me so much that I completely forgot.

"Why are you demons here? I highly doubt you've been asked by the guild to come here, right?"

"It's this." With her fork, Beelzebub pointed to the meat.

"No, that's too weird. There's no way you could've known we were going to have a barbecue party here."

Though it was possible that demons had some kind of precognitive power.

"No, no, we didn't plan on barbecuing here, but we were planning on using boar as an ingredient for the demons' food."

"What?! You were?!"

The strength of Laika's flames got briefly hotter the moment she heard that, almost scorching Flatorte's clothes.

"Yes. We knew that there were too many long-hammer boars in this region, so we came up with a plan to use them as food and take them to the demon lands. We were here today to investigate. And the humans living here would probably be overjoyed for it, so two birds with one stone, no?"

"I see... I didn't even think about that...," I mused.

"In my leviathan form, I can carry roughly a thousand boars altogether. We could even butcher the meat on board on the way to Vanzeld Castle."

Vania used the term *on board* to refer to her own back. Apparently, she saw leviathans as boats.

"You're going all in... If you could hunt boars on that scale, then they'd no longer be a threat to people."

I felt like human countries would end up much better managed in that case.

"Demons eat a lot, you know. We have to effectively take any extra meat. We also once hunted deer in an area where they had overpopulated."

"Lady Beelzebub is the minister of agriculture, so she often deals with food problems like this."

Wow, so that's Beelzebub's real work!

These sorts of problems fell right in the description of Beelzebub's job. It wasn't like she was being paid to do nothing but arrogantly proclaim she was the greatest in the world.

"You were thinking something rather rude about me just now, weren't you...?"

"...Nope, you're just imagining things."

She's pretty sharp...

Flatorte's clothes were finally dry, so she put them on for the first time in a long while.

"This is the power of culture! I feel like I've become smarter!"

"That comment makes you sound like a complete idiot, yet you still have experience leading the blue dragons, so please pull yourself together."

Laika sounded ashamed that her rival was acting this way.

"I think I'm a bit jealous of her taking off her clothes. That's not really an option for ghosts."

Living with us must have awakened Rosalie's sense of fashion. I suppose I could teach her some magic to change her clothes when we had time.

Now that Beelzebub and Vania had joined us, the meat started disappearing faster, but there was still a good amount left.

"Hey, Beelzebub, what should we do with this?"

"We need more people. I see we have no choice but to call on Falfa and Shalsha."

She didn't mention Halkara, but it wasn't out of malice; it was only because Beelzebub absolutely adored my two daughters.

"You're right. We were going to get them to come anyway."

"Yes. I can guarantee they'll be safe, so you can call on them as much as you like. Anything that threatens them will be eradicated just like those boars!"

I appreciated her intent, but I'd rather she kept the eradicating to a minimum.

"My love for them will quickly surpass yours if you let your guard down."

"Don't worry about it, since that'll never happen. My love for them is like a bottomless spring that's about to…no, that *is* overflowing."

This was the one thing I couldn't budge on, as their mother.

Sparks flew between us as we stared at each other.

I actually wished she wouldn't try to outdo a mother's love. Couldn't she concede on that point?

"I—I'm not saying you've failed as a mother or anything, okay…?"

Good. Beelzebub was backing down.

"Anyway, it's true that we need more people. That's how I will approach this," she said.

"Right. And if you find anyone you can invite, just bring them on by."

Laika looked at me, then nodded with a smile. "I will now shuttle them over."

"I'm sorry for making you do this right after you've eaten, but thank you."

"Certainly. The landing spot I use as a dragon is a little ways away from the village, but I can still make it back without losing much time."

"Fantastic! See you soon, then!"

Among the ones remaining at the site, Vania was absorbed in developing a new menu, thinking about different dishes for different parts of the boar.

"The head bumps on these long-hammer boars look like they might have a unique texture. We can cut them into cubes, heat them, then add herbs to make a salty-sweet sauce."

"What? That sounds amazing!"

"Then, we'll cut gaps into some bread, pour the sauce in, and eat that. Would you like a taste?"

I didn't have any reason to say no, so of course I'd eat it.

Yep, it was delicious. I knew it would be, but it was really good.

I was starting to get full, but this stomach still had room!

Flatorte was just taste testing, but she had seconds anyway. "I am *so* happy right now!"

"Those words are the greatest compliment a chef could ever receive!"

Vania struck me as the scatterbrained type, but I saw her in a completely different light now.

Halkara was the same; she was a force to be reckoned with when it came to the things she was passionate about.

As we sat around, the moment we had all been waiting for finally arrived.

Laika in her dragon form returned with Halkara and my two daughters.

"We were going so fast, I was starting to get scared...," Halkara was saying.

Shalsha's expression was also vaguely miserable.

And on the flip side, Falfa was in high spirits. "We came right away! It was a big adventure!"

I could see how different their personalities were. It was like the difference between who would and wouldn't enjoy a thrill ride.

"All right, everyone! Let the barbecue party begin!" I said.

"Yay! Falfa's gonna eat a whole bunch!"

"Shalsha's ready to eat, too."

"I'm a vegetarian, but I still love a good party!"

Just as I was thinking about how nice it was that the whole family was here, Beelzebub appeared behind them. She must have used some kind of teleportation magic.

"They would get angry with me if I didn't invite them, so I brought them along," she said.

One of the people behind her was Vania's older sister, Fatla. She was the one who'd carried us when we went to get the Demon Medal, and she was the one who took care of us on the way back.

Fighsly, the Fighter Slime who had started training under Beelzebub, was also there.

And the last person, with those characteristic sheeplike horns—

"This is a dream come true, to feast with my darling elder sister!"

"Oh, Pecora. Long time no see. But it feels like I've been seeing you a lot anyway."

Pecora swiftly closed the distance between us and wrapped her arm around my waist.

She was a rather powerful fighter, so if I ever relaxed my guard around her, she'd always end up in my personal space like this.

"You smell absolutely delicious, Sister."

"Er, don't say weird things like that. Have some nice meat instead..."

Once again, we resumed our barbecue party with even more people.

There were plenty of options now that Vania's dishes were also in the mix.

It had become a much more cultured ordeal now, considering how our original goal was just to eat some meat.

The new members of the party had natural smiles on their faces.

Shalsha and Fatla were chatting about something, no doubt forging a new friendship. They were both the levelheaded type, so I was sure they were on the same wavelength.

There had been a cynical time in my life when I thought normie events like a barbecue by the river were completely pointless, but that wasn't true at all.

"Mistress, isn't eating meat so worth your while?" Flatorte was smiling, her plate stacked high with so much meat that it seemed a little too much for her stomach.

"I wish you'd sit and give a long think about a few things today, but—I'll let it slide for now."

That was because I was starting to enjoy the whole affair.

It wouldn't be very convincing if I lectured her with a smile. Today, we would just enjoy a great time together.

"We should probably get back to hunting boars, so we'll do another pass with Beelzebub and the others this time."

"Yes, mistress!"

And so, we killed even more long-hammer boars. So many of them.

We froze them with Flatorte's Cold Breath and sent them off with Vania in her leviathan form.

The boar population had been significantly reduced, and the guild thanked us.

$$\diamondsuit$$

A while later, I learned that demons would go out to hunt whenever there was an increase in animal populations—not just long-hammer boars but deer and other types of boars.

It was a fantastic deal; it wasn't just plain old charity work, but it was also to gain food and help the regions struggling with these problems.

And there was an increase of something else in my yard.

There was a small cover on the ground, and taking it off revealed a ladder.

At the bottom of the ladder were rows of frozen meat.

Yes, the cold cellar was a new addition.

We were mostly storing meat for now.

In the past, we could chill foods either by using my magic or Flatorte's Cold Breath, but since it took up so much space, we only really ever used it for food that was already prepared.

But now that I knew some among us were big eaters, I set aside a space just to store meat in earnest.

"Phew, it's so nice and cool in here. I would definitely get excited about this if I had this as a kid."

We also hunted boars and deer for our own personal consumption when the population got too high, and we stocked them here.

"I should bring back some venison for dinner."

My repertoire of boar and deer dishes was growing significantly. *Maybe I'll ask Vania to teach me again.*

Then, I heard a strange rustling sound.

Someone can't be in here, can they? It's not like the place is locked or anything, though.

It was at times like this that I got scared despite my high level.

No matter how high my stats were, a girl was still a girl. I hoped it was anything but a pervert.

It wasn't entirely impossible that a wild animal somehow got inside, but there shouldn't be any animals that could manage that around here. We were a little ways from the forest. Oh, could a slime have gotten in somehow?

The cellar was spacious.

I slowly went in deeper.

Again, I heard the rustling sound. It didn't seem like I'd misheard earlier. I decided to take the plunge and stepped right into the cellar.

"Who's there? I won't allow any trespassing!"

There stood Laika, her back to me, doing...something.

"Oh... Lady Azusa..."

Guilt was written all over her face. She was doing something that she had to hide, for sure, but I couldn't exactly tell what that was.

"What on earth are you doing? I won't get mad, so just tell me. Well, it's not like there's *no* chance I'll get mad, but I'll try my best not to, so tell me."

Laika turned around timidly, gripping grilled meat in her hand.

And then I could smell the aroma. Had she grilled it with her fire breath down here...?

"Are you...snacking?"

She nodded once. There was no way she could deny it, since I'd caught her in the act.

"I got hungry, and I knew there was lots of meat down here... I'm sorry..."

I could even hear a mean rumble coming from her stomach. Had she really been that famished?

"Fine. I'll increase your food expenses. Then you can eat much more than you are now. You're not on a diet or anything, so it's fine."

"Thank you, Lady Azusa!" Laika bowed her head, the meat still in her hand.

"Of course. No need to hold back now."

Laika bit into the meat.

"Don't tell me you've been going hungry this entire time?"

"No, that's not it... I just felt like having a snack, that's all!"

She vigorously shook her head in denial.

There was no mistaking that she was embarrassed because it was improper.

Looking at it another way—she was munching on a hunk of meat for her afternoon snack?

I still had a lot to learn when it came to what was common sense for dragons and other races. She shouldn't have to be so defensive. I was sure that I would never hear the honest opinion of the more reserved types, like Laika.

"Okay, then I'll leave my cooking duty for next time," I declared. "Instead, we'll all go to the Savvy Eagle and eat our fill! You can order as much as you want and stuff yourself!"

We headed to Flatta and dashed to the Savvy Eagle.

"We'll start with ten omelets; and rabbit steaks for all of us, so six of

©Benio

those; and another six salads— Wait, what do you mean you don't want one? Come on—you have to!"

Shalsha said she didn't want a salad, but she had to consider her nutritional balance.

"It feels like things have gotten very lively all of a sudden..." The shop owner was astonished.

"We've changed the way we think about our meals. We're still growing children, after all."

It was times like these where we would ignore how long we'd lived. We *looked* like we were growing children, so we were.

If we ended up getting fat, well, we'd cross that bridge when we came to it. Time to stuff ourselves!

Flatorte didn't seem entirely satisfied yet, and she was staring diligently at the menu like a student cramming for a test.

"Mistress, can I have this goose dish?"

"Of course you can, Flatorte. Order as much as you'd like!"

"Mistress, how about the lamb?"

"Of course you can. Your body may be slim, but your spirit can be full and plump!"

"Mistress, it sounds like they have turtledove in stock. Can I have that, too?"

"...Now I'm not so sure if the money I brought will be enough, but worst-case scenario, I'll just have them bill me, so go ahead!"

It wouldn't be a big deal if Laika was the only one, but now there was someone else who ate just as much. I could already feel the pain in my wallet...

"You should have more self-control... Can we have the goose, lamb, and turtledove dishes as well?"

In the end, Laika also ended up ordering all the same extras that Flatorte did. I had to force myself not to comment.

I spent more than seventy thousand gold that night, but we had a fantastic time, so whatever!

Laika and I spent the next day killing move slimes than usual.

Clang, clang, the break-time bell rang.

"Phew! Time for a quick rest."

I stretched out my arms and headed for the break room, then flopped down on the sofa. There were only a few people who worked the morning shift, so I had the sofa all to myself.

Halkara entered the room. She always wore this jacket-like thing over her clothes when she was working as the company president.

I might have been imagining it, but it looked like her expression was kind of strained.

"Thank you for your hard work this morning, Madam Teacher."

"Yes, you too. Phew, sometimes work like this is good for me!"

"But don't you get bored of it? Wouldn't a more creative field be more suited to your experience and skills? You don't have to be here just for such simple labor..."

"But it's actually kinda fun to get into simple work!"

"Well, it puts a lot on my mind when you're here, so I would prefer if you stayed at home, like usual!" Halkara was being honest, so she was serious.

"Aww. Shouldn't it be easier on your mind to hire someone you know for a part-time job instead of a complete stranger?"

"Well, maybe for a younger sister of mine. But you're my teacher,

Madam Teacher! I have to be much more attentive if someone of a greater status than me is working at my factory!"

That's right—I was actually working part-time at Halkara's factory.

I wasn't in need of money, so I was really just killing time. It had been quite a long while since I actually wanted to do something work-like.

By the way, the job I'd been doing until just a few minutes ago was sticking labels onto the products that the company sold.

No conversation, just making sure there were no wrinkles.

"Man, you know, I've gotten pretty good at sticking the labels on. None of them was on crooked, and I think if I kept going, I'd be a master at it."

"You really don't need to go that far... If you want to aim high, then please do so with medicine... Personally, I would be much prouder and happier if that's how you earned your greatness, Madam Teacher."

I see. I mean, I understood what Halkara was trying to say. She wanted me to do something where she could genuinely respect me. But—

"If I was to become a top-tier herbalist, I'd have to travel far and wide on foot to discover herbs. That sounds like a huge pain. And it's not like I can drag the whole family along with me, so I'd be alone..."

What made me sad was that I'd have to leave my beloved daughters and family behind and take up work on my own.

And if I did become a legendary herbalist, requests from nobles and the rich asking me to cure their diseases would come in from all over the world. I'd get way busier.

You couldn't build a laid-back lifestyle on that.

That's when Halkara said with a blush, "That's true. We'd hate for you to leave us." *Why did she blush there?*

"I like taking things little by little. I don't really feel like gaining power, even as an herbalist or a witch. The other part-time workers just think I'm a girl who lives nearby anyway."

That was when an older lady who also worked the same shift as me came in and said, "Oh, Miss Azusa! Lovely to see you."

There weren't photographs or anything in this world, so even if the name of the Witch of the Highlands was well known, many people couldn't match the name with a face.

Halkara looked like she was trying not to say anything. She probably didn't really like that I wasn't being worshipped, but my desire for recognition was fulfilled enough in the area around Flatta.

Once that boundary started expanding, it would never stop.

"Hey, Azusa, do you have a crush on anyone? Shall I bring in some prospective husbands for you?"

"Oh, no, that's all right! I've actually got two daughters already."

"Wha…? I see… Ha-ha-ha…"

Once I mentioned I had daughters, conversations like these stopped immediately.

People often said I looked really young, so it was the most glorious way to put an end to that.

"Oh, that's right, have you heard about the great Witch of the Highlands?"

Of course she'd bring up the Witch here.

"I live near Flatta, so I've seen her in the flesh several times."

I played along innocently. Halkara would probably want me to say, *That's me!* though.

"I hear the great Witch is traveling around the entire country. She truly is a great woman!"

Wha—?

I feel like I've just heard the beginning of an impossible tale…

"Oh, that's the first I've heard of it…"

"I hear she vowed to cure the world of illness and is walking from land to land selling medicine. Living legends truly are on another level!"

"I—I see… But I saw the great Witch of the Highlands near the village today… I wonder why that is…"

"There's a dragon child at the great Witch's place, no? Couldn't she just have ridden her to come back?"

Oh, so that was the only part she knew well. I guess dragons were a separate topic.

"Well, I'm going to grab a bit of water. Bye-bye, Miss Azusa!" the older lady said and left the room.

Halkara and I were the only ones left. We inevitably looked at each other.

"Halkara, this isn't good…"

"Madam Teacher, I can't believe you never told me you were doing something so virtuous."

"I'm not."

I couldn't possibly have told her. Because I wasn't doing anything of the sort.

"It means there's a fake out there pretending to be me. She probably knew her medicine would sell better if she used my name."

"Who…? Who would do this…? This is unforgivable… We must demand compensation for the psychological distress caused by this!"

Whether or not she would pay damages was a different matter, but it was true that we needed to do something about it.

If this fake did too much work, that would put me in a bind, and if she committed a crime or did anything to lower my reputation, that would just bring the negative consequences to the real Witch.

"Okay, we'll sue her in court."

"Being the president of a company really makes you choose the proper adult course of action, doesn't it, Halkara…? But we can't do anything if we don't know where the defendant is. She's traveling around, so we don't know where she lives."

Halkara looked at me in agreement.

"So first, we'll give this fake a good earful ourselves."

$$\diamond$$

When I got home, I held a strategy meeting.

"—Which basically means there's a fake me out there."

"Utterly unforgiveable." (Laika)

"We'll string her up!" (Rosalie)

"I'll kill her." (Flatorte)

"If we follow precedent, we can be sure she'll serve five years in prison." (Shalsha)

"Yeah, you're my only mommy." (Falfa)

It was starting to sound pretty gory in here, but I wanted to administer a less-harsh punishment if possible.

"Either way, we won't get anywhere if we don't gather any information. I guess we should head to a faraway province to ask around. She's a fake, which means she has to tell people that she's the Witch of the Highlands. That basically means she can only work in places where no one knows the real thing."

Which meant the fake should be somewhere far away from here.

"Lady Azusa, isn't this a time to ask for help from the demons?" Laika offered a constructive idea. It would be effective to have more people searching, but…

"Sorry, I think I'll pass on that… Those guys do things way too thoroughly…"

If the demons ended up coming to town to investigate, "the Witch of the Highlands" might just end up "the Demon of the Highlands."

"For me, I just want this to end peaceably. I'd honestly be satisfied with the fake earnestly reflecting on her actions. But of course, if she's been selling medicine that doesn't actually work, then she should be punished."

Selling fake medicine was fraud, and in a worst-case scenario, someone could die. That's when she'd end up in court.

"Then can I ask each of you to search for info on this fake on your own?"

And that was how we began our hunt for the imposter.

Laika and I decided to ask around in a town in the west.

On the other hand, Flatorte flew off to the east.

I didn't think I was very well known in the south, but I'd won a tournament the other day, so now I was famous there. That probably wasn't an easy place for the fake to work. It was unknown if this imposter had any experience in battle, but people usually didn't want to be randomly asked to spar.

So for now, our strategy was to investigate everywhere but the south.

"Oh, right. I feel like it's been a long time since we've asked around or gathered information."

It's a pretty standard thing in RPGs, but it wasn't a common task for people unless they were adventurers.

There was a game series called *The Ark*, and I remembered ignoring the main story line and instead working on side quests from the guild. The main story line was really dark, so I had to take more breaks from it than usual. Well, that didn't really matter anymore.

"If we're to ask around, then how about a tavern?" Laika suggested. "I'm not very fond of them, since they're usually teeming with ruffians, though."

"Or a guild, because there might be drifting adventurers there. One of those, I guess. We'll need patience for this, so we just have to keep our heads up as we go. Okay, I'll go to the guild across the river, and you take the tavern nearb—"

Laika was tugging at my clothes.

"I...do not do very well in places like taverns, so...if you could come along with me, I would be most grateful..."

Aww, she's so cute!

"Laika, you're a proper lady, aren't you? You don't like spots full of drinkers, right? Then I'll go with you."

"But, Lady Azusa, my question is, why are *you* fine in places like that?"

"Because I used to fall asleep in cheap bars that would be open until late—or early morning, whatever you want to call it—then head in to work the next morning..."

Now that I thought about it, those days really were the worst. It's no surprise all that work killed me.

And old guys who sexually harassed girls also hung out in the taverns of this world. If Laika went in on her own, it wouldn't end well.

The tavern was on the larger side, even for the capital of the province, so there was still quite a crowd during the daytime.

"Hey, pretty lady! Step on me!" "Please, call me names!" "Glare at me and say I'm the worst!"

"Why are all these vulgar catcalls so masochistic?!"

Then, a female employee with a sharp glare approached us.

"Welcome to the public tavern, A Pig Would Be More Useful than You."

This was definitely more in line with a gimmicky bar than a public tavern.

"Hey, miss, another drink, please!"

"Shut up. Go to the kitchen and get it yourself," said the employee. The concept of customer service had been thrown out the window.

The perception that the customer was always right was a bit much, but there was something wrong about treating them as lesser than pigs.

"See, Lady Azusa? I don't really deal with places like this very well…"

"Trust me, Laika, you shouldn't treat this place as a standard for taverns."

"This shop was about to be shut down a long time ago because the employees' hospitality was so awful, but when they started anew and made the rough treatment the focal point, it immediately flourished. A little change in perspective won the day, didn't it?" said the employee with the sharp glare.

That was too much of a change.

"It doesn't seem like you two are here for our special brand of rough treatment. Did you want to apply for a waitress position?"

I wouldn't be caught dead working here.

"We have a question for you, but I'd hate to ask for something without giving anything in return, so I'd like to place an order."

"If you want to return the favor, then could you taunt those men over there? If possible, it would be best if you acted disillusioned or uncomfortable, like you were looking at something dirty."

I can't believe we found ourselves in a place like this!

Oh well. The employee looked like she had a lot of information, so I would go along with what she asked, just for a little bit.

I did my best to look as ticked-off as possible.

"Missy, we want to order more!"

"Don't talk to me when you reek of alcohol."

"Missy, we also want—"

"You *want* to get kicked. Is that it? Quit flapping your gums."

"Maybe I should order an expensive drink?"

"The water in a horse's bucket is good enough for you."

"Missy, how 'bout a smile?"

"…I'm sorry? Did you just tell me what to do?"

I wondered if I was doing okay, but some of them were tearing up with delight.

These people are bonkers!

"Ooh, being insulted really does feel great…" "This is exactly what I walked three hours here for…" "Ooh, I got the shivers!"

Laika said, "I want to disinfect them with flames." *I know how you feel, but please don't burn them.*

"Thank you! Now the financial support will come rolling in thanks to those pigs!"

The employee finally outright compared the customers to pigs.

"Now, ask me anything you like. I'm pretty confident when it comes to information."

But still, it wasn't like she would know right off the bat.

"Has an herbalist calling herself the Witch of the Highlands been around here?"

"The Witch of the Highlands? Yes, she has. I think she even stayed in this town."

She did know right off the bat! She had every right to be confident.

"We're looking for her. Please tell us about her; anything is fine!"

"Well, I haven't seen her. I've been dealing with these drunk pigs here, after all."

"The customers might chew you out if they hear that. But I guess that's why they come here, so never mind…"

You could say she was still thinking about work even when she was talking to us.

"Once, a new employee called a customer *sir*, and he lost it. *What the hell; don't behave modestly like that!* he said."

This is way too twisted. This world is doomed.

"One of these drunk pigs may know something. You can ask them if you like. They can speak human language."

I still can't believe we came to a place like this…

Laika and I posed our question to a few of the old men who were good and drunk.

"Do you know the Witch of the Highlands?"

"Yeah, I do. She's that witch, from the highlands."

"You don't know anything!"

"Hey, nice jab! Be meaner about it, though! Like, *You're worthless*, or something!"

"You *are* worthless!"

"Aah, that's great! I get stressed when my wife says it to me, but it's like a compliment when it's from a young girl!"

I bet his wife would have a few choice words for him if she found out he was coming here…

Laika had seemed bewildered by the old men at first, but something in her had snapped during this whole ordeal, and her gaze had gotten colder.

"Silence, puny humans. You dare speak to a red dragon in such a manner? Do you wish to be ripped to shreds?"

"Whoa! This is my first time seeing this type! More, please!"

"Such filth has no right to request anything from me."

"Thank you! Thank you!"

Laika, don't forget, our whole point of this is to ask about who the fake is, okay?

In the end, no one there had seen the Witch of the Highlands herself. They were all worthless (which is an expression I'd use only for this tavern, since I'm normally a milder person).

Then, we decided to ask if there was anyone who had bought medicine from the witch.

If she was selling harmful drugs like poison while using my name, it would not only affect others' lives but also my position. This was the one thing I wanted to check before anything else.

On the other hand, if she was selling a bunch of useless junk without any medicinal value, then someone who needed medicine might end up taking something ineffective and die without a cure.

"Well, my wife went out to buy cold medicine from her, but the witch said, *My position doesn't yet allow me to sell curatives*, and apparently didn't sell her anything."

"Huh, that sure is a commendable thing to say…"

I was relieved to hear she wasn't selling medicine, but I was mad that the imposter just decided to lower my reputation…

Come on. I can make cold medicine…

"Right. I hear that she didn't sell any medicine in other lands, either. Apparently, she said she didn't want to earn money on her fame alone."

While what the customer said gave me relief, the mystery only deepened. If she didn't need to earn money on fame alone, then why was she acting as my fake?

I was almost certain that she was selling fake medicine to get rich quick. I mean, what other reason was there?

Not knowing what she was after gave me a bad feeling.

"Lady Azusa, the Witch of the Highlands left on a road heading north two weeks ago. If she is staying in every place along the way, then she might not have gotten very far."

"Thanks, Laika. Then I guess we can follow her."

It was a big relief even just getting an idea of what to do next.

"Are you leaving already?" The employee approached us. "If you like, you're welcome to come back and work for us again. Your wages would be five times what you'd earn in a normal tavern."

I'll bet. That definitely wasn't the salary for someone working in a bar...

First, we went to the outskirts so Laika could turn into a dragon, then we headed to a town sixty miles to the north.

Incidentally, *miles* wasn't really a unit of measurement in this world, but I still had a habit of converting things in my head. Here, the units of measurement were slightly different depending on the region, so it was hard to keep track.

It would take a (very average, not someone like Laika or me) woman about three or four days to travel sixty miles by foot. The people in this world had stronger legs than those of twenty-first-century Japanese people.

And if she stayed two or three days in the town along the way, then I figured she would be right around here.

I began my questioning at the greengrocers near the town square. The fake was probably hoping for attention, so she would likely come to the town square.

"The Witch of the Highlands? Yeah, she was just here two days ago. But she was different than I thought she'd be," said the lady at the shop.

We were closing in on the fake! But I wondered what she meant when she said she was different than she'd thought.

"I heard through the grapevine that the Witch was more of a beautiful young woman. But she wasn't like that at all."

"Oh gosh, well... I don't really pay much attention to my beauty. It might just be the climate."

"Why do you look so happy? Though I guess you are a pretty one."

"Ma'am, I'll take some of those apples and oranges."

We had to contribute to the shop's sales. It was a given, since she gave us some good info.

"Lady Azusa... Are you sure you're not buying too much...?"

"It's fine. I can eat plenty of fruit, no matter how much we have!"

I regretted it a little when I lined up all my apples and oranges at the inn.

"We can't cook when we're traveling, so I think I might get bored of this…"

"Lady Azusa, you sure are vulnerable to flattery." Laika seemed scandalized, but she soon started chuckling in delight again. "But I am happy to have seen that side of you."

"In my past life, I died from overwork before I was recognized for anything… I'm avoiding things that'll make me too conspicuous, but I mean, I'm still happy when someone compliments me. There's nothing to feel guilty about."

"Indeed. As your pupil, I truly respect how you keep nothing from others, Lady Azusa. I might even say that it's an ideal way to live."

Well, that was a nice thing to say!

And now that I thought about it, this was my first time traveling alone with Laika. Had I started on an aimless journey, this was probably what our life would have been like.

"All right, as a reward, I'll give this to you."

I held out an apple.

"I'm tired of it already. I would prefer some meat…"

◇

We switched up our search for the fake and continued on foot. As long as we silently walked along, we'd catch up to her sooner or later.

"We'll check every settlement as we find them. If there's a crowd gathered in one of them, that'll be our answer."

"Understood! We will absolutely catch her!" Laika was more enthusiastic than I was.

And then we discovered a suspicious crowd at one settlement.

I called out to someone near the back.

"Excuse me, what is all this for?"

"The great Witch of the Highlands is here! How thankful we are!"

We had finally caught up to her.

Laika and I slowly made our way through the crowd. I guess our first job was to see how she was acting and what she was saying.

And there she was—a decrepit old lady.

Her back was practically hunched over at ninety degrees, and she was even gripping a cane.

I felt like the bend in her back was much more of a problem, though.

She definitely wasn't a beautiful young woman! She wasn't young at all!

A beautiful witch, then? No, that didn't work, either. No matter how I looked at her, she wasn't beautiful.

Lovely old lady? No, I thought *lovely* was pushing it once you reached the decrepit stage.

She was feebler than I thought, and her stretched skin hung down—it was all rather peculiar.

"Ho-ho-ho-ho. Ho-ho-ho-ho-ho.

"Ho-ho-ho," the fake was saying. Actually, that was all she was saying.

"When you have energy, you can do anything. Ho-ho-ho."

You don't have any energy to begin with! You look like you're gonna collapse any second now!

"I am the Witch of the Highlands. For roughly three hundred years, I have lived in the highlands."

That was the same as me. But of course it was, since she was plagiarizing me.

"The great Witch is incredible." "She is so experienced." "There's so much to gain just by looking at her." "Are we sure she's not undead?"

The people watching were all saying whatever they pleased.

One of the audience members raised their hand. "Why are you traveling at your advanced age, great Witch?"

"I am collecting yet unknown herbs and traveling the country. Ho-ho-ho-ho. Even yesterday, I went through the mountain pass from Melte to arrive here."

"But isn't it hard going around the whole country on foot? It'll take so much time... And wow, I'm impressed you got through the mountain pass at all."

I thought I saw the old woman jump slightly in response.

"Yeah... Now that you mention it." "Even a horse has a hard time getting through that pass." "But an undead would be fine, right?"

Yes, good! Doubt her, audience!

"When you have energy, you can do anything!" the imposter yelled, opening her eyes wide.

There was her aggressive technique!

"I see, as long as you have energy, huh?" "Energy is important." "The undead need energy, too."

She was sweet-talking them.

And I was really starting to wonder what happened to the person who kept mentioning the undead...

"Then what's the secret to energy?"

There came a question. But this fake didn't seem to have any energy at all, no matter how hard I looked.

"To not die."

Another thoughtless answer!

"She's not wrong." "We're winners just by being alive." "Because the undead don't die, y'know." "Will you honestly shut up about the undead already?!"

She's really pushing it... And someone in the audience finally complained about all the undead comments!

Then someone from the audience said, "Please sell us medicine!"

Talk of the Witch of the Highlands's medicine should have spread to this region.

I made a living killing slimes, so I sometimes forgot, but a witch's main line of work was pharmaceutical.

These could be health brews or strange-looking substances filled with lizards or scorpions, but either way, my main job was making those.

Laika also seemed to understand that this was an important point and tugged on my clothes. It was her signal for me to pay attention.

Now, fake, how will you respond?

"…I have not yet reached a level in my training that allows me to sell medicine. Once I have matured more, I will sell."

"No way!" That was when I raised my voice and interjected. "You've been doing this for three hundred years, right? Then how long do you need to do this to be independent? The world of witchcraft isn't so severe that you'd stay a novice for five hundred years!"

"Lady Azusa, they'll notice you; they'll notice you!" I was about to lunge forward, so Laika intervened.

"It's fine; she's a quack anyway. It's not like she's selling anything, so I'm not obstructing her business at all."

Then I went all out on the offensive.

"I heard that the Witch of the Highlands was young, so then why are you so old?" I stared at her thinking, *You're so fake.*

The imposter's expression read, *This is bad…*

"Oh yeah, I heard that the Witch of the Highlands was a beautiful young woman." "Apparently, she looks seventeen." "Tch, so she's not undead…"

The audience seemed to realize that something was odd.

"I heard she's the most beautiful in all of Nanterre." "No, I heard she's the most beautiful girl in the kingdom." "Yeah, no man can look at her without falling in love." "She's glowing with a bright light all the time and stuff."

You guys are getting carried away! This will make it too hard to reveal who I am!

Well, even if I didn't reveal myself, I could still give this fake a good lesson.

"I am Liliri the Witch. And, by the way, the Witch of the Highlands is my friend. I'll be straight with you—this old woman is a fake!"

The name I used was, of course, a false one. I didn't need to say I was the Witch of the Highlands here.

The fraud hunched over even more than before. She was definitely trying to avoid eye contact.

"The young girl said that." "She's cute, so it's probably true." "Yeah, she is cute." "It's almost like she's undead."

People were agreeing with me for the most random reasons.

And whoever that was who likened me to the undead? Rude.

"If you're going to keep calling yourself the Witch of the Highlands, then show us proof that you are. Let's have a magical sparring match. The Witch of the Highlands would never lose to me."

I went straight in and asked for a real fight. Testing people wasn't a very good thing to do, but it wouldn't help if news of the fake's loss didn't spread.

"Hmm... Very well. I've made up my mind."

Oh, are you gonna do it? It's not fun if you don't. Sorry, but I'll show you what I'm made of.

The phony witch suddenly straightened out her back...

Then immediately bent it again to ninety degrees.

"I am a fake! I am sorry!!!"

"Now you're hunched over because you're bowing?!"

I ended up commenting on the fake's very graceful response.

"What, she's a fake?" "She's not a beautiful young woman, of course." "But I thought she was undead." "Dude, your obsession with the undead is really weirding me out."

The audience dispersed.

I guess that was fine. Well, the fake was an old woman, so it would've been cruel to hound her for further answers. She wasn't gaining profits by swindling others in this region anyway.

But we stayed, because this was when the real deal began.

Laika slowly approached the fake.

"I am Laika, apprentice to Lady Azusa, Witch of the Highlands. I heard there was someone pretending to be my master, so I was searching for you. Why have you decided to act out such a lie?"

"…My back hurts."

She was clearly trying to dodge the question!

"That is odd. When you bowed earlier, your back stretched out fine."

Laika the detective… She was conducting a thorough interrogation.

The fraud must have thought it was inevitable, because she stood up straight at attention. Laika's deduction was correct.

"Please forgive me…" Her voice sounded somewhat younger. Of course she couldn't have traveled in such a feeble body.

"Then can you answer my question? Why did you decide to make yourself into an old lady? The Witch of the Highlands is known to be a much younger woman."

"That's…because I ended up getting into it without really knowing the details… I learned that the Witch of the Highlands was young after I started doing this…"

"That sure is a half-hearted attempt at impersonating someone!"

I had the same impression when she was explaining to the crowd, but people who did stuff like this didn't often plan very well…

"Now a question from me. Why did you take the name of the Witch of the Highlands? And without even selling anything? There's nothing to gain by assuming a fake name like that, then, no?"

Yeah, I was wondering the same.

Without any means of making money, then the risks of being a fake stood out much more. She might not have expected the Witch of the Highlands's apprentice to show up, though.

"Honestly, that's the biggest question. I have to ask to understand why."

I wanted to know the culprit's intention. In cases like these, it was unlikely that the culprit did it because she suddenly lost her head, so it wasn't an unmotivated action.

And if the reason was rational, then we could also be careful to make sure that a second or third fake didn't appear. Or if it was a sympathetic reason, then we probably could allow for extenuating circumstances.

"Er, well... You know... See, it's a common thing..." She was having a hard time coming clean, which convinced me that there was something shady going on for sure.

"Spit it out, or I'll drop you into the mouth of a volcano from the clouds," Laika threatened with a straight face.

"I'll say it; I'll say it!"

All right, we'll finally find out why. We'll have her say it loud and clear.

"The reason I became the fake Witch of the Highlands is..."

""Is?!"" Laika and I said simultaneously.

"...because I wanted to be pampered!!!"

The answer came out of left field—out of a completely different dimension of reality. I just stood there blinking.

Laika looked even more confused and stared at her almost as though she hadn't heard.

"I'm sorry—I don't really understand what you mean. Could you provide more detail?"

Answering must have taken a lot out of the old lady, because she slowly slipped down to sit with her legs splayed out on the floor.

When she was in this form, we looked bad, since we weren't helping her out. I wanted her to turn younger if that was what she truly was.

"Um, I've been a witch for a long time, too, but I'm not in the public eye at all... And I wanted to be noticed, so I took on the name of the Witch of the Highlands. But I thought she might track me down if I walked around selling medicine, so I pretended I wasn't that skilled in medicine yet so that I didn't have to sell any."

"Please don't try to distract us with such nonsense details. I am not a very kind person, so I may spew fire at you." Laika didn't think her reasons held water. "In the end, the Witch of the Highlands will get all the credit for anything you do, not you. And your true name will remain unknown, so it makes no logical sense!"

"Laika, wait, wait! That's a fair argument, but it's true that there are people like this in the world..."

I was pulled back to a memory of my past life, of jerks who presented pictures other people drew as their own.

And while that absolutely was plagiarism, it wasn't done for money or for fraud, so it was rather difficult to punish them.

There were probably people like that in this world, too.

You know those old guys at public taverns who say stuff like, *Hey, I'm pals with that minister*? If you pester them for more details, it turns out they just happened to pass him on the street. This was pretty similar...

Even if there was no actual benefit, people would lie for their fifteen minutes of fame.

"I suppose I'm having a hard time understanding. That wouldn't improve your skills at all, would it, fake? Even if your improvement is slow, you may grow stronger if you act as yourself. This is illogical. Are you giving up on yourself?"

"Laika, she looks like she's about to cry, so we should probably stop with the logical arguments soon..."

Laika was a big proponent of personal growth, so she probably couldn't fathom this...

"I—I'll show you my true form."

The elderly lady suddenly transformed into a young redheaded girl.

By normal standards, it looked like she suddenly de-aged sixty years.

That said, there were way too many beings in this world whose looks and ages didn't match, including my family, so the girl's true age was a mystery.

"I am Eno, a witch... I have the power of immortality, but I've been living in obscurity for almost a hundred and fifty years... A terrible voice told me that I might hear some positive feedback if I became a fake..."

A hundred and fifty years…

I couldn't deny the possibility that such a strong desire for recognition could drive someone crazy after all that time.

"Honestly, you lack humility. My master, Lady Azusa, would never look smug, no matter how strong she is."

Laika was in lecture mode, as always. Ever the serious one.

"The difference in strength between you and Lady Azusa here is that attitude!"

Whoops, she blew my cover… That was a bad way to put it…

"Oh, you mean this girl here is Azusa, the Witch of the Highlands?"

Laika's expression gave it all away. I really wished she'd wipe the guilt off her face.

"Well, she's been found out now, so I suppose I should just tell you. This girl here is Lady Azusa, Witch of the Highlands!"

"Laika, at least try to bluff!"

We still could've gotten away with it, right?!

And so we identified the fake as a witch named Eno.

We also revealed that I was actually Azusa, Witch of the Highlands…

That day we listened to Eno's story at the community tavern, and it was an intense one. I started to sympathize with her a little.

"I'm a witch, but no one knows who I am… I don't have any friends, either… I don't have any hobbies, and I always think about how empty existence is living as a witch…"

"Aah, that's what happens when you're immortal with no friends…"

In my past life, I had read plenty of books where an immortal character couldn't bear the loneliness anymore. That was truth, in a way.

"But, Lady Azusa, why have you been fine on your own for three hundred years?" Laika instead directed the question to me.

"Hmm, now that you mention it… Well, I had contact with the people of Flatta, and they started to admire me during the three hundred years I sold them potions, and my desire to be recognized was fulfilled."

"I knew it; your humility truly is marvelous! It would not even be impudent of you to call yourself the strongest in the world with your power! I have rediscovered how wonderful you are, Lady Azusa!"

"Laika, you're getting something wrong here! I only recently realized my stats were so high!"

There wasn't a single person out there who aimed to be the strongest by killing a few slimes every day.

"*Sigh*... If I had any interests that I really wanted to succeed in, then I probably wouldn't have acted as a fake... *Hic*..."

Eno looked like the sad-drunk type, and she was constantly looking down.

"You have to have one or two points of pride, right? You're a hundred and fifty. I bet there are people out there who think you're great at something."

"No, you're too optimistic. I'm really just a nobody... I'm a totally nameless witch... I'm not involved with the witching industry or anything like that."

Well, I don't know anything about a witching industry.

But the thought of neglecting her gave me a twinge of unease.

When I was in college, I'd listened to the troubles of one of my junior members in our club but couldn't give any good answers, so she ended up leaving.

*Which, by the way, was really just a club for fun. All we did was play Ping-Pong at hot springs (and not even at hot springs).

Of course, there were some troubles that only the troubled one themselves could fix. That being said, I felt like this would've gone better if I had been more amiable toward her.

"Then, Eno, take me to your witch's workshop. I'll find something you're amazing at there."

"Wait, you're coming to mine, great Witch of the Highlands?"

"Yes. People often can't identify the great things about themselves unless someone on the outside points it out to them. If I find something wonderful about you, then you can let that be your driving force in life."

In short, I figured I could just search for Eno's good points. Hopefully she'd take pride in whatever it was. If she could stay motivated, then her long life would become more enjoyable.

"Very well… I doubt you'll find anything interesting about my life, but if you say so…"

"Then it's settled. I look forward to it."

We were going to visit the house—well, workshop—of my junior witch.

$$\diamond$$

The next day, we flew on Laika in her dragon form to the land where Eno lived.

"There isn't enough space for a dragon to land, so I hope you don't mind landing a little early and walking the rest of the way."

"Oh, sure. I'll leave that to you."

My house, which sat right in the middle of the highlands, was special. That turned out to be a good thing, since two dragons ended up living with me. It would be a pain to walk fifteen minutes just so they could turn into dragons.

"Go straight here, then once you see the road, turn right. Then turn left at the next junction." Eno directed us as we headed to our destination.

It was a spot pretty deep in the mountains, one where a dragon could touch down only after a great deal of trouble.

"We'll walk from here. Follow me."

We entered the forest after Eno. It was rather gloomy.

"This place is a little uncanny. In a way, it's the environment you'd expect for a witch."

"Yes, I chose it because I thought a proper witch should live in a witchy sort of place."

We followed the red ribbons tied to the trees along a path that could barely even be called a path.

I would have no idea where we were supposed to go if it wasn't for these markers.

"I should've worn more comfortable clothes. These are going to get dirty..."

"We've been walking around in the woods and mountains a lot lately, haven't we...?"

Laika wore Gothic Lolita–style clothing, so I bet she was having a rough time.

And the path was long. There weren't any sudden uphill slopes or anything, but the woods were getting thicker, and it was getting darker. I could hear the ominous *kee-aw, kee-aw* of a bird echoing around us.

Also around us were several types of valuable-looking mushrooms that would make Halkara happy.

After walking for twenty minutes, Eno announced, "We're here."

It was just an empty wood.

"Sorry. If this is a joke, I don't get it; there's no building here."

"We go down into the grotto from here."

On closer inspection, there was a tunnel that we could probably squeeze through if we crouched down.

"Seriously...?"

"Oh, no need to worry; I'll use some Light magic."

That wasn't really the problem.

Laika and I squatted and made our way through the tunnel. After about five minutes of wriggling like caterpillars, we found a small rope ladder.

"And now we go down."

"...Okay, sure."

And after climbing down the ladder for several minutes, we arrived at Eno's secret base–like workshop.

There was also a double lock on a metal door, which made it look especially like a secret base.

TRESPASSERS SHALL BE CURSED was written there.

That probably loosely meant, "No solicitors." I highly doubted anyone would come all the way out here just to make sales, though.

"I've stayed in here for over a hundred years, but my name hasn't spread at all..."

"Well, duh!"

No one would ever find this!

Some shops were like hideouts, but you could take it too far.

"And are you going to town to sell your potions?"

"No, I make them as a hobby, but involving all my time in business activities doesn't strike me as very witchlike, so I don't. I figured if I made something good, word would spread quickly..."

"That's not gonna make you famous!!!"

This girl's desire for attention really did not match up with her work ethic!

We entered her workshop. It was a dreadful place, one that practically screamed out *Witch*.

Bottles with lizard tails and scorpions dipped in mysterious liquid lined the shelves. And various animal bone specimens hung on the walls.

"This is an eerie place..."

Laika was shrinking away, apparently not fond of places like this. I felt like some people would be more afraid of dragons than this stuff, but that was a different source of fear.

"Oh, please, have a seat."

There was a set of table and chairs, but the chairs were also made of bone.

It doesn't look very nice to sit on, so I think I'll pass...

"Don't you find it weird that you want to be like me? I think our styles of witchcraft are way too different..."

"No, because I'm making medicine, too. Like, for example... this one."

She took a bottle down from the shelf. Instead of liquid, it contained a few small pellets.

"These are pills made from dried Mandragoras. They're effective in relieving fatigue. They also do wonders for the eyes and settle the stomach!"

"Hey, that's not a bad thing you've made there."

Afterward, Eno talked at length about how she made the pills and showed us a dried Mandragora.

"All these Mandragoras have been aged three years, and I use ones that have been carefully grown. I can make the medicine from younger versions, but then the components aren't at their fullest potential. And so as a potion-making professional, I can make it without any compromises!"

I was also somewhat of a witch, so once I heard how she made it, I could at least tell that it was a well-made concoction.

Thinking about it rationally, if she was immortal, she was among the exceptional witches. She couldn't be just some unremarkable girl.

"This is pretty good. I bet it'd be a big hit if you called it the Mandragora pill and sold it. Or wait, are you selling it already?"

"No. I believe a proper witch shouldn't carelessly allow herself to be known, so I do not put things on public sale."

"What a waste..."

"W-well... It's not like I haven't thought of it. If someone recognized how good these pills were and asked to turn them into product..." Eno bashfully fidgeted and looked down. "See, if a witch comes out and announces she's selling something, that would be too merchantlike, too out of line for a witch's way of life... I've always wanted to be, like, a genius for those in the know, you know...?"

Oh. I think I've mostly figured out how she's making things more complicated for herself.

"You want to be in a position where only the top witches of the world would recognize your work, if you could, right?"

"Yes. I would love to be someone who only sells medicine to people I acknowledge and to turn away witches who come to me without referral!"

Eno's eyes seemed to shine a bit.

"And so, as the very stubborn craftsman you are, you want to be more well-known by the world, right?"

©Benio

"Yes, right—that's right!"

"Isn't that a little contradictory?" Laika interjected from beside us. "You only want to be recognized by people in the know yet want to be acknowledged by the whole world—I don't think you can accomplish both. Is this something only alchemical philosophy can solve? I am uneducated, so I don't quite understand."

Laika's voice was like sharp thorns.

If I could hear what her heart was saying, I'd probably hear it whispering, *You idiot.*

And it seemed like those words reached Eno.

"Well… It's just as you say, but… But you know… What I mean is—"

"What you mean is what?" Laika quickly closed the distance between the two. "Your behavior has been completely inconsistent this entire time. What is it you hope to accomplish? What do you wish to do? Will you please explain so that fools like myself might understand?"

I thought I saw Eno hunching over. She seemed pretty defeated.

I clapped my hands.

"That's enough, Laika. I'll explain in Eno's place."

"You can make sense of such difficult logic, Lady Azusa? Brilliant!"

Well, I wasn't genius enough to "make sense" of it; I think we just need to assume that humans are inconsistent beings to begin with…

"Hey, Laika? Humans have appearances to keep up."

"Vanity, you mean?"

Well, don't just say it. Then it gets a little too real…

"In Eno's case, she wants to come across as a cool witch. To be more specific, a genius witch available only to those in the know, without any sort of commercial flair."

Eno nodded slightly. I guess she was embarrassed about admitting it.

"On the other hand, she wants to be known throughout the world as a great witch. But in order to do that, she needs to make good potions and advertise them for sale, and even though she lives in this kind of hidden workshop, no one is coming out here to find her."

If only she'd be active a little closer to places where people actually lived…

Not even her fellow witches would be able to find her in a hideout like this. And if other witches couldn't find her, then word of her work wouldn't spread throughout the trade.

I thought she was too thorough when she decided to start with appearances.

"That is a mystery. I can only see it as a contradiction."

"No, she definitely is contradicting herself. Actually, you could even say that someone whose words and actions did match up was peculiar. And since you're never too unsure about anything, Laika, it's probably harder for you to understand."

Eno silently listened in to our conversation the entire time, her eyes trained on the ground.

"This is just my opinion, so if you have any counterarguments, speak up, okay? What I just told Laika was a generalization."

"Th-that's not wrong, though… I'm sorry…"

If the girl herself was aware of it, then the rest was easy.

"So basically, you just want people to fawn over you, right?"

"Yes, I do!"

"And what do you think you should do to accomplish that?"

"My only choice is to do things that will make me famous!"

Right, well put.

"Then we'll get to doing those things."

Eno seemed a bit frightened by what I said. "Um… When you say do *things*… What exactly should we do…?"

"Sell potions. Sell them and put your name out there."

"Th-that's… Well, I get terrible social anxiety with strangers, and even though I'm fine when I'm disguised as someone else, I am so nervous and completely useless when I'm not…"

So that was why she'd seemed fine when she was disguised as the "Witch of the Highlands." Plenty of people become outgoing once they start acting, so I understood somewhat.

"We'll get used to that, too, as we go along. Doesn't it suck living in such a lonely place, hidden away from other people?"

"Yes... It does... I want more attention, and I want everyone to gaze at me in admiration! And if possible, I also want a bronze statue of myself! I want to be named an honored citizen in my hometown!"

And now she's a fountain of worldly desires!

"But now that I think about it... I should have put my workshop closer to a city. If only I was in a place with easy access to the kingdom capital..."

"Lady Azusa, this girl is suddenly starting to change her approach... Are we sure she hasn't summoned an evil spirit and let it possess her?"

Laika was surprised about it, but in a way, this was the result of Eno being honest with herself, so I wanted to praise her.

"No, this is fine. It's perfectly fine that she feels this way. All right, let's get selling!"

◇

We went to the nearby village and bought the rights to open a stall at the big market they held there once every two weeks.

Opening up her own store right away was too big a hurdle for her, but preparations for appearing at the market were comparatively few. And even if she got tired, she could go home and just sleep until the following day.

And so our table number was A-23b.

"Yay, a wall!"

Eno was happy. A wall? What did that have to do with anything?

Now that we knew where she was going to be, we started making our setup for the products and advertisements.

It was a little embarrassing, but we made a flag that said, MANDRAGORA PILLS—THE WITCH OF THE HIGHLANDS'S CHOICE! I really did think they were good, so it wasn't a lie.

Laika prepared the change and other smaller details.

It was at times like this that I saw how considerate she was. In the future, I knew she'd make a good wif— Actually, I'd want her to be one of my little sisters.

"Lady Azusa, I have a sign that says, FIRST OPENING! and a banner that says, ONE HUNDRED AND FIFTY YEARS OF EFFECTIVENESS. Shall we use either of these?"

"Laika, you never do anything by halves…"

But all three of us worked together to finish the initial preparations.

"I think most everything should be ready by now. We're going to go home for a bit, and we'll be back on the day of the market."

"Okay, thank you so much! I will aim to be the number one in pill shares!"

I feel like she's leaning too much toward the commercial side, but whatever…

Then, the day of the market arrived.

Laika and I came to attend.

The spot was facing the wall of a big building, and since there were no other tables behind hers, she had plenty of extra space. So that was what she'd meant by *wall*. Well, she wasn't wrong.

We went and saw that Eno was already there constructing her spot like a pro.

It was a much more serious affair than when we had been helping her. It practically looked like a permanent store.

But there was something else that stood out way more than her construction.

Eno herself—and her really gaudy outfit.

She wasn't wearing witch clothes but something more like a baby witch. No, wait. A magical girl. The witchlike black motif was nowhere to be found, and her main colors were more pink and white. She even had a staff— No, a magic wand.

"Hmm… This is a new sort of heresy…"

As a resident of a fantasy world, Laika's worldview was making her cautious.

"Eno, I'm not in a position to pretend like I don't know you, so let me ask—what is all this?" From the perspective of an ex-Japanese person, this looked 100 percent like cosplay.

"See, I told you I was socially anxious, right?" Her voice was very crisp and high-pitched, like an anime character. "So by taking on the role of a completely different character, I have conquered my embarrassment!"

"I see. I don't really know if this is right or wrong anymore, but if it satisfies you, then that's perfectly fine!"

"And this outfit is based on fairies. This land's tales of fairies date back centuries."

So it *was* cosplay.

In front of her shop was a sign I didn't remember us making that said, First Bottle Half Off—Today Only!

That's fine. You do you!

"I prepared five hundred bottles for this day. I hope to sell out."

Behind her was a stack of boxes that probably had the bottles in them.

It would be terrible if she was left with excess stock...

"Isn't five hundred right off the bat a little overconfident...?"

"I can do it; I can do it! I almost considered making a thousand."

Eno spoke with sparkling eyes, but I thought, *This kid's gonna end up disappointed...*

If she couldn't sell out, then it'd all end up in storage... And it'd just be a manifestation of the truth that they couldn't sell, plain as day to the exhibitor herself...

No, I shouldn't be thinking about failure right from the start.

Then, it was ten o'clock. The market was open.

"Welcome! We have Mandragora pills from the Witch of the Deep

Mountains! Mandragora pills, they're good for your body! They're the Witch of the Highlands's choice! Yes, today your first bottle is half off! You can buy them at half price! Come one, come all!"

Her advertising voice was loud.

"Lady Azusa, I don't think we need to be here... She is doing this all on her own..."

"You're probably right."

The pills stood out from the wares of the other shops around her, so they were garnering some attention, but would they sell...? However, when I saw how serious Eno's expression was, I knew this had been the right choice.

"Laika, look how hard this self-effacing and shy human is working. I think we could call this a success at this point, right?"

Someone who had spent all her time waiting for someone to notice her was moving more and more into the spotlight.

"And even supposing this is a failure, she can use this as a spring to keep moving forward. So I know she'll succeed someday."

Laika seemed to understand what I was saying and nodded slightly, but—

"So does that mean you are expecting her to fail this time around?"

"...W-well... It looks like she's getting some attention, though..."

It was time for the day's market to close.

Eno sold seventy-three bottles of Mandragora pills.

I didn't really know the rates for stuff like this, but I thought she put up a good fight for her first time.

Still, Eno was staring blankly at the remaining four-hundred-plus bottles.

"Where should I put these...?"

"We'll have to put them in storage somewhere."

"How odd... I did so much advertising, though..."

I thought she did *too* much advertising, which made it hard for people to stick around. I even heard people say, "Why's she dressed like that...?"

"I'd say you did well enough. You had newsworthiness, and you had some customers who like bizarre foods come just for that. I'd say it was much better than not advertising at all."

Laika gave her objective comments.

Right, if Eno was going to fail, then it was better she did so after doing something rather than failing by not doing anything at all. The experience would lead to the next opportunity.

"First, I need to think of what I'm going to do with my excess stock... Maybe I should dig another cellar..."

"I can help you with any hard labor. I dug a cellar next to my house in the highlands, after all."

Eno looked defeated for a while, but by the time we were done dismantling and packing things away, she seemed cheerful.

"It's fun standing in front of people and selling them things. Whenever I received money, I was glad that I was doing this."

"Eno, that means you're fulfilling your desire to be recognized in a respectable way."

"Huh?"

"People giving you money to get something you made yourself means that they've acknowledged you. All you have to do is keep on keeping on."

"Y-yes, okay! I will keep going!"

Eno's eyes glittered. *Yes, devote yourself, young witch.*

"Next time, I'll join the fight with an even higher-quality outfit!"

"Wait. That's not the point of this."

Since she had also been acting as a fake Witch of the Highlands, I would call this girl a costume enthusiast.

There were probably plenty of ancient festivals all around the world that involved dressing up, all of which probably appealed to humans' instinctive idea of fun.

We managed to fit the remaining bottles in an extra room and didn't have to make an extra cellar.

"I want to go into town more without staying cooped up in my workshop."

"Yeah, that's a good start."

"And when I have the chance, maybe ask people if they'll buy my Mandragora pills…"

Yeah, the excess stock would get in the way after a while…

"You just need to think about this positively. Imagine how rough it would have been if you made a thousand bottles."

As I listened to Laika's comment, I thought, *Let's not make product in the four digits right off the bat. She should see how things work out with three hundred at most.*

"I'll buy one of your extras. How much are they?"

"Oh, no, I'll gift it to you! Or, actually, please, take one! It's free!"

I ended up taking two bottles for the house. As a witch, I could give its effectiveness my seal of approval.

"We'll come to see you again."

"Yes, I'll be waiting!"

My protégée energetically waved her hand.

"Please don't pretend to be the Witch of the Highlands anymore, okay?"

"Yes, from now on, I will be the Witch of the Grotto! I will be participating in the market for a little while, so feel free to stop by!"

◇

And so, we peacefully solved the issue with my fake, but there was a little more to the story.

One day, a little over two weeks later, a letter came to the house in the highlands.

The sender was Eno, so I opened it, expecting a report on how she was doing.

Dear Lady Azusa,

I'm sorry... I know this is sudden, but the Mandragora pills suddenly flew off the shelves at the following market... I can't keep up with production at all...
I want to hire someone to work with me, but I have no experience, so I don't know where to start... What should I do...?

Eno, Witch of the Grotto

What, the pills were a hit?!

I went to Eno's to hear what she had to say.

Someone who bought the pills last time used them and felt much better. This spread by word of mouth, and apparently, many others vowed to buy some, too.

In the end, all the leftover stock she'd brought because she had nothing to lose sold out at the next market in the first two hours, then soon after that, she was swarmed with orders. Now pill production was bearing down on her.

"I need to harvest good-quality Mandragoras, but I have no time to go out..."

"This is a matter for Halkara. I'll have to ask her."

I sent Halkara out, and we explored the possibility of mass-producing it, but since making the pills required a special technique, there were limits to that.

Eno, having given up on that avenue, made the medicine made-to-

·order and sold only as much as she could make. She was apparently known as the "medicine-making artisan" for about three months after they sold.

Since I'd managed to extract the hidden talent inside her, I thought I had done well.

Now the Mandragora pills made by the Witch of the Grotto sat in my room as my household medicine.

FLATORTE

A blue dragon girl who obeys what Azusa says. Since she's a dragon like Laika, there is somewhat of a rivalry between them, but she's an optimistic and energetic girl. Unlike Laika, she has a tail in human form.

"I AM IN NO MOOD TO BE FRIENDLY WITH A RED DRAGON!"

ROSALIE

A ghost girl and resident of the house in the highlands. She's devoted to Azusa, who didn't shy away from her as a ghost and instead reached out to her. She can go through walls but can't touch people. She can also possess others.

"I'LL FOLLOW YOU FOREVER, BIG SIS!"

PECORA
(PROVATO PECORA ARIÉS)

The demon king. A girl with a devilish temperament who loves to use her power and influence to bewilder her subordinates and Azusa. She actually has a masochistic desire to be subordinate to someone stronger than she is, and she adores Azusa.

"HOW WONDER-FUL IT IS TO HAVE A COOL WITCH FOR AN ELDER SISTER!"

When I woke up in the morning and left my room to have breakfast, I noticed the population had increased considerably.

I wasn't surprised to see Beelzebub anymore, but I wondered why both Vania and Pecora were here.

"Oh, Sister, good morning," Pecora spoke, elegantly sipping on tea.

"Why is the demon king here so early in the morning? This isn't your castle, you know."

"There is a profound reason for it," Pecora responded boldly.

The reason the dining table looked much more refined this morning was probably due to the presence of a nation's leader. There wasn't much in it for me, though.

"No, Your Majesty, our reasoning isn't that deep. Today we're on a quest in the area, so we decided to pay a visit while we were nearby," Beelzebub lightly corrected her.

"Yes. We knew you wouldn't be out and about at this hour."

Vania's comment sounded selfish. Well, it wasn't a habit of ours to eat out in the morning, but maybe that was the problem.

Halkara brought over salads dressed with bread fried and then chopped up. It must have been a hassle for the person in charge of food to suddenly have an increase in people to feed...

"All right, here are the extra salads... Is this enough?"

"Yes, it's delicious. A crisp salad in the morning wakes you right up, doesn't it?" replied Beelzebub.

Flatorte, who preferred a hearty breakfast, looked like she had something to say. "Well, how we feel about breakfast doesn't really matter—"

"Sister, I baked some cookies."

Pecora produced some cookies and held one out to me, so I opened my mouth. She placed it inside.

"This isn't just something a girl made for fun; this is a pro-level cookie..."

"Yes, the cooks at the castle taught me how to make them."

She sure was lucky to be in an environment where she could select the best teachers.

Falfa and Shalsha also reached into the cookie box and munched away.

They weren't that bad for their health when compared to fatty foods, so I figured they could overeat just a little.

And when the two dragons had some free time, I'd ask them to make some cookies again.

"So what business brings you here toda—?"

"Here, Sister, have another. This one tastes a little like strawberry."

I opened my mouth again. And right in went the cookie.

"Mm, the fresh strawberry taste really fills your mouth."

"Wonderful. I will apply myself even harder!"

"These cookies are absolutely delectable. It's a deliciousness that is incredibly hard to put into words."

Shalsha's stiff compliment for the cookies sounded a little odd, given her expression. She was probably just saying how good they were.

"Yeah. The crunch is very nice, but it doesn't dry out the throat and has the perfect amount of moisture to it. I think they're incredible."

For some reason, I spoke very highly of them without cracking a smile.

But our main topic right now wasn't the cookies.

"I believe that none in the lands around Vanzeld Castle would be able to beat Her Majesty's cookies! I guarantee it as a chef!" Vania had given her seal of approval, but she was sitting a bit farther away from Pecora, so she was definitely scared of the demon king.

"Yeah, I can sense a hint of wheat in the cookie. It's very soft, too, and since they're so light, I could eat a great number of them. That aside, why are you here tod—?"

"Yes, I also brought stone bread, a local specialty of my hometown."

Beelzebub set down a heavy-looking piece of something that looked like bread. It was almost the size of a human face.

"Halkara, have a taste. Take a bite from this part first."

"I won't be able to eat this all on my own if you don't cut it into pieces. But I will do as you say and try it."

I was impressed by Halkara's lack of aversion to unknown food.

"Oh, it's sweet; it's so sweet— Ah, now it's getting spicy. Something weird is going on in my mouth!"

"Yes, yes. There are a variety of different flavors mixed in to stone bread."

"You can enjoy all the different flavors if you eat it slowly, but taking a big bite like that creates a battle of flavors in the mouth. It's a refined taste."

Vania expressed some positive thoughts, but I wondered if that was good enough for the demon chef.

I guess it was like one of those giant Japanese rice balls with the different kinds of stuffing inside. Taking a big bite of one would put *mentaiko*, seaweed, and pickled plums in your mouth all at once.

"Ooh... I need a sip of water... It may not be to my taste, but it is interesting."

Halkara was thinking positively.

It was really possible that her way of life was bringing her success as a businesswoman. Even if something was bad, she was never discouraged.

"Halkara, was it? Your salad is delicious, too."

Pecora smiled at Halkara, but perhaps because of everything that had happened in the past, her smile was a little strained.

"Well, I suppose we should be off to work soon. Please head back home, Your Majesty." Vania was trying to give up on the spot.

"Wait, wait! What work did you come here for anyway?!"

I finally got to ask.

When the demons were working, it was hard to say that what they did would have no impact on our world. Since I was a concerned party, I wanted to at least ask. I had to stop them if they were liable to stir up a lot of chaos.

Beelzebub pointed to the ceiling.

There, Rosalie was floating.

"What? Does this have something to do with me...?!" She was shocked.

"To do with ghosts, somewhat. And yet, as a general rule, ghosts don't typically cause concerns where we would intervene."

For some reason, she was starting to tell it to me like a riddle. Well, you don't get to do this every day, so I decided to play along.

"So things related to ghosts would be, like, a bogey or a zombie?"

"Yes, you're getting warmer."

I just threw those out there. Did I get it right?

"In one word, the undead. We're looking for an undead."

"Ghosts don't have physical bodies, so they're outside the demons' jurisdiction, but the undead are a different story. Whether they are demons or not is a gray area, but demons protect them because it doesn't seem like there is any management over them in the human world."

Vania's explanation was pretty easy to understand. She was right that there were no laws about the undead in the human world.

But I braced myself a little when I heard that word: *undead.*

At the very least, it struck me as more dangerous than the troubles that came with too many boars.

"So, are we sure this won't evolve into a big disaster...? Because don't humans turn into zombies or whatever when they get bitten...?"

"Why does being bitten by a zombie turn one into a zombie? Zombies aren't a plague," Beelzebub retorted. "And by the way, *zombie* is considered offensive to the undead, so you should be careful. They're unhygienic, but they live on demon land nowadays."

It sounded like *zombie* was apparently the word for the unclean undead.

"Humans sometimes use magic to turn themselves into undead. It must be a part of experimentation as they try to become immortal. And so that's how the undead come to exist in the human world." Pecora answered my question before I could ask it.

"I see, so the undead are born from the human world. And so when someone becomes undead, then they're taken care of by the demon side."

"Yes. If humans discovered there was an undead among them, they may start to fear it at best, and at worst may burn it alive. The walking dead don't have rights under human law, after all."

There definitely wasn't a law anywhere that said the dead had a right to a trial.

"We received a report from a demon who went shopping in the human world that they spotted something that looked like an undead," said Beelzebub. "This business shouldn't have anything to do with me, since I'm the minister of agriculture, but…I'm here because I received an official appointment to search for this thing. I often come to the human world, so I *must* be used to it."

"Yes, I asked her." Pecora smiled devilishly. No need for the *ish*, though, since she was literally the demon king.

But I was thankful, too.

When I thought about the risks completely different demons might pose, my anxiety lessened knowing that my acquaintances, Beelzebub and Vania, would be doing the searching.

"And so we'll be conducting our investigation in this region, starting now. It's rather tricky because the information we got was vague and difficult to narrow down… It might even be in a completely different province… Most demons don't have a very firm grasp on the geography of the human world…"

It must be like if a Japanese person heard the name of some obscure place in America—they wouldn't even know where to look.

Beelzebub looked so done with her work, and she hadn't even started it.

Looking for a single undead in an unfamiliar land sounded like some kind of punishment game.

"Oh yes, I just thought of something." Pecora clapped her hands together.

Both Beelzebub and Vania were filled with dread. She was always toying around with them...

"Why don't you help us out, Sister? I'm sure our search will be far more productive with your help."

"Wow, that's a rather good idea coming from you, Your Majesty."

For every degree Beelzebub's expression brightened, mine clouded over.

"Wait, why me...?"

"It's not like you have any regular employment, do you? You'll be rewarded."

Don't talk about me like I'm a bum with no direction in life! I am making a living, off killing a few slimes every day!

"Right, if a human found the undead first, they might kill it," said Beelzebub. "Maybe you say you won't mind if an undead dies. Or perhaps that something not alive is better off dead. I see; I see."

"Urgh, it's unfair to make it sound like its life depends on me... And what you're saying really scrambles my brain..."

So are they dead or alive? Can you please be clear about this...?

"Fine, fine, I get it. I'll help you out, okay?"

"Hmm, you should have said so from the beginning."

She sure was quick to change her tune, but Beelzebub seemed a bit happy about it, and I doubted she had bad intentions.

"Everyone, you can all sit this one out. I've personally agreed to help the demons on my own. Carry on with your day as usual."

Falfa replied, "Okaaay," and then the rest of the family seemed okay with obeying my orders. This was probably fine.

We had just recently searched for my fake; we were doing a lot of manhunts lately. Maybe this was what they meant when they said, "When it rains, it pours."

"What sort of distinctive characteristics do undead have? I've never seen one before, so I don't really know."

"Nothing in particular."

"Nothing in particular."

Both master and servant breezily gave me a terribly useless reply.

"Then how are we supposed to find it?!"

"Instinct."

"Instinct."

Do they know I'm a guest in their party, here?!

Things were already looking pretty grim for the near future…

$$\diamondsuit$$

After asking a little more about the undead, I learned the following:

- The undead are indistinguishable from humans by looks alone. Those who appear to be rotting, like zombies, are very few.
- But since their dead bodies smell, many use fox perfume to hide it.
- Those who originally had jobs as members of society often wish to keep that status.

This will make it a pain to search…

We met up with Vania's older sister, Fatla, and Fighsly joined us as well. Since Fighsly had come with Beelzebub as her pupil, it felt like she was being used however Beelzebub wanted, but since she was a slime to begin with, she probably didn't mind working under a demon.

"We will now begin our search for the undead. I hope you will all put in your greatest efforts."

Beelzebub sounded like a leader giving instructions.

"By the way, how are we going to search for this thing?"

"We will ask around at random if anyone has seen an undead."

I guess since demons lived such a long time, they were fine with spitballing options until something eventually worked out…

◇

We first went to Flatta and went around asking this:

"Excuse me, we are undead collectors. Please let us know if there are any in your vicinity. The undead are people, too. Please refrain from burning them alive(?) and hand them over to us instead!"

"The Witch of the Highlands is up to something strange again." "Oh, great Witch, how do we tell the undead apart from regular people?"

The villagers started to gather around us, so it was easy to ask.

"We've heard that there might be an undead in the area. It's harmless, but we don't want anything terrible to happen to it, so we plan to take it into our care." I explained with very simple reasoning.

"Please let us know if there is anyone among you who wears an obscene amount of perfume."

"Oh yeah, my wife's perfume drives me nuts." "Yeah, you get close to her 'cause it smells good, only to find a monster!" "She'd punch you both into next week if she heard you!"

They sure were easygoing. I doubted there were any undead in Flatta.

Then, the sky went dark.

Fatla had turned into a leviathan and was flying overhead. It could've been Vania, but the quiet, elegant soaring was definitely Fatla's.

She was hard to ignore, as always… There were villagers who were staring up in awe. It was a massive creature, after all, so they probably weren't used to it.

Then, something fell from Fatla—pieces of paper, or something like it, fluttering down from the sky.

I picked one up, and it read:

Man, the demons really were sloppy!

And I wondered if they would be okay entering the human world so blatantly.

"Wow. That's a huge animal!" "Mommy, can we keep it?" "How are you gonna pay for its food?"

The people of Flatta were well behaved, weren't they? I guess my living nearby was part of the reason for that...

And so Fatla's strategy of distributing flyers reached every corner of the province itself. One area apparently panicked and sent out the army, but the arrows didn't go high enough to reach the leviathan, and since she just flew off, the whole commotion died down.

But once the day was over, I complained to Beelzebub at our finishing trip to the tavern.

"Was there any point in my joining for this...?"

"Of course there was... To explore and gain information on the local area by yourself is also very important..."

Could you please look me in the eye and tell me that?

"If someone learns something, this way, we should receive a report. It is indeed a good and sensible way of doing things." Fatla looked somewhat confident.

I'd acknowledge that about the plan, but there was no reason for us to be here.

"I am so tired from running all over the province and handing out pamphlets… I almost thought I might turn back into a slime…"

Fighsly was out of fuel, and she had her face resting on the tavern table.

This shouldn't count as training.

"It's painful, but I must get stronger… Then I can earn even more money…"

Her motives were so selfish!

"The food at this establishment is not very good… Their preparation is unsatisfactory. Even though the very same ingredients could be made into something much more delicious… The chicken skin isn't crispy at all…"

Vania the chef was complaining the whole time. Apparently, there were some things she just couldn't let go.

"Well, we've covered considerable ground. Now finding the undead is but a matter of time."

Beelzebub the leader was merrily drinking her alcohol and fanning herself, as though we'd already won.

This had turned into a strange debriefing…

"Azusa, come tomorrow, just in case. I believe we will find our target sometime tomorrow."

"Yes, yes. I'll treat it like a part-time job."

But against Beelzebub's expectations, there was no word about any undead.

We handed out flyers in nearby provinces as well, but no response.

"We've come to a dead end…"

Fatla, who was probably a perfectionist, was getting paler.

As usual, we finished the day at a tavern in some town.

It looked like members of the demon race really liked these end-of-day meetings.

"The possibilities I can think of are, one: there was no undead to begin with, or two: the undead is out there somewhere, but it's hiding. If it's the latter, then the flyers won't be very effective," I said.

"Hmm... We spent quite a bit of money on the pamphlets, so I do hope they'll be effective... I fear the officials at the treasury will nag me..." Beelzebub sounded worried about what people at home would say. "Come, Azusa, don't you have any good ideas? I know you'll think of something!"

"Come on! Don't praise me when you need something from me. We don't even know if it exists in the first place, so the hurdle is way too high for me."

It was very possible we were searching for something that didn't actually exist.

"What if we added a reward to the pamphlets? Like, fifty million gold to anyone who finds it."

"We don't have the budget for that, Fighsly, and if we did, people like you would lie and say they found it."

I thought she was being too harsh on her apprentice, but Fighsly's face tensed, so they were both to blame.

"Um... Would you happen to know anything...? You are the most knowledgeable about human lands, Azusa...," the pale Fatla said to me.

"I haven't heard a single peep about unde— Wait, yes, I have."

Where was it, again? It was pretty recently that I'd heard the word...

I certainly wouldn't have been talking about the un-liveliness of the undead myself nowadays, so I had to have heard it from someone else.

But no one in my family was interested in the undead. I didn't think that had been a hot topic in Flatta, either.

So if it wasn't at home and it wasn't in Flatta, then there were only a few places left... *Oh, I remember!*

"It was when I was looking for my fake! There was someone who was weirdly obsessed with the undead!"

I didn't remember getting a clear look at the person's face, but that was all I had.

"Couldn't that just simply be an undead fanatic?" It didn't sound like Beelzebub trusted me yet.

"I don't think that's a thing. And even if they were, someone that enthusiastic about them would probably know where one was."

$$\diamond$$

The next day, we headed for the community where I found the person who wouldn't stop referencing the undead.

We started by asking around. If only I could remember what they looked like... I had a feeling it was a woman, though.

First, we visited the person who looked like the village leader.

"What? No, you won't find something so terrible in a pastoral community like this. Why, a sheep catches a cold here and makes the news!" the mayor said leisurely. Hmm, our first shot was a miss.

"Fear not. This is a small community. If we ask everyone, it will become clear in due time," Beelzebub said to me and started asking. The population of the place really was small enough that questioning every single resident was possible.

I asked everyone I met about the undead, but by the time morning turned to noon, we had no results.

"Undead? No way, not here." "I've never seen a rotting person before."

That was strange. Did we come to the wrong community? But this was the place where I found the fake, so I didn't think I got it wrong...

"Well, this was a complete failure, wasn't it?"

Beelzebub was staring at me hard. And she wasn't the only one. Fatla gave a tired sigh, and Fighsly was hitting her legs to make a point, it seemed.

"W-well, what can we do...? Stuff like this happens..."

Then, a lady passed by with a basket filled with apples that were very—maybe *too*—ripe.

They must have smelled a little rotten, because there were even a few flies buzzing around them.

That caught my attention.

"Excuse me. Aren't those no longer edible? I have heard that they're most delicious just before they rot, though."

"Oh, these? They're for Pondeli, who's currently acting as the grave-yard watch."

"The graveyard watch...? I'm sorry—I don't follow; do you think you could tell me more about it?"

"The graveyard watch is a little bit of a joke, you see. She's essentially a grave-keeper. See, the community graveyard is up on that hill over there, and Pondeli has been watching over it for five years now."

Beelzebub was taking high-speed notes behind her.

"Word is, she has a strong stomach and has said she can eat things that have started to rot with no problem, so I bring them to her often."

"I see! Do you mind if we go with you?"

We headed for the public graveyard. According to what I heard from the lady on the way:

"Pondeli casually wandered into town about five years ago. She said she'd act as graveyard watch. We told her we don't have any graves of royalty with hidden treasure or people who would mess with the graves, but she insisted, saying, *No, I'll watch over them! I don't need much income, either!*"

So she asked for pay? What a cheeky girl she was.

"She doesn't seem like a bad kid, and she has been taking care of the place under the name of the graveyard watch. She's told us that her professional eyes will keep the graves safe and sound."

What sort of skill was that...? Maybe she could quickly find and clean dirt on the stones that a layperson couldn't or knew how to make offerings without attracting crows.

But the words *graveyard watch* really stood out to me...

I was reminded of the poor souls from my previous life that regularly got stuck with the *graveyard shift*. Never again...

We finally reached the top of the hill. There was a small hut for the manager at the entrance.

"Pondeli lives there."

She would probably be suspicious if we all suddenly barged in on her.

"Ahem, this girl here, Vania—she actually loves looking around at graves… They call it 'graving,' see. She is particularly interested in the graves of famous people, so we'll go ahead and look at the graves if you don't mind!"

"Huh? I don't give a lizard's tail about gra— Mgggh!"

Her older sister, Fatla, covered her mouth. *Great job.*

"I don't think we really have any graves of famous people here. The only one might be the one who won an orange-eating competition. His headstone is in the shape of an orange."

That might actually be worth giving a look. I really wanted to see it.

"Oh, she's right! There's an orange one here! And it's not just a relief; it's a freestanding orange! An orange statue!"

Vania was the most excited about it, and she ran over toward it.

You really are *interested!*

We let Vania go running off to the graves, and we gave the lady some space so we could confirm who this Pondeli was. She would probably come out to see the woman.

"Azusa, do you think it's an undead?"

"It might be. The undead don't age, right? Which means it sounds like she'll go from place to place to live, right? People might get suspicious if they saw how she always looked young and never aged."

Then the door clicked open, and a girl in her pajamas appeared.

She had a cat's ears and tail—she must have been a catperson.

"Pondeli, I brought you your rotting apples."

"*Yaaawn*, thank you. I'm sorry—my days and nights are backward, so I just woke up. I was playing games all night…"

"You really do lead an irregular lifestyle, don't you? You need to eat. You're looking pale again today, too."

"I'm fine. I eat when I'm hungry and I sleep when I'm sleepy. I am devoted to nature."

There was no doubt about it.

I didn't know if she was undead, but she was definitely a NEET...

And on her pajamas, it said: *I'll end up a magic stone if I work.*

Meaning, probably: *I'll die before I work...*

Once the lady left, Beelzebub knocked on Pondeli's door.

But there was no answer.

"Hmm, perhaps she doesn't open the door if she doesn't know who it is. Security-conscious, this one," Beelzebub commented.

"It's fine. Leave this to me."

I could sort of see how I could deal with this.

"Hello, there's a package for you! I need your signature!" I called in a pitch somewhat higher than my usual one.

"My apologies, but I think this idea might be too much..." Fatla looked doubtful, but this would be good enough.

"Wouldn't saying something like, *We discovered a small magic spring that gushes holy water* be better?"

"Fighsly, that sounds like a water purifier scam..."

"Oh, I just thought of something else. Couldn't we make a killing if we used that as a reason to increase her monthly bill?"

"I think you're going to be arrested sooner rather than later..."

That wasn't something someone who devoted themselves to the martial arts should say...

And my package strategy was a success.

The door clicked open.

"Books sure do come quickly nowadays. Thank y— Huh?! Mraw?!"

She saw our faces and must have instinctively realized she was in a bad spot. The sound she made was very catlike, as befitting a catperson.

She tried to close the door, but Beelzebub had already twisted her hand into the gap in the door and was forcing it open. No one should underestimate the power of a great demon.

"Heh-heh-heh. Are you our undead? You are, aren't you?"

©Benio

"N-no! I'm just a regular graveyard watch! I watch over the grave-yard twenty-four-seven!"

"Oh-ho, then perhaps we should take you to the temple and have the cleric there cast some purification magic on you. We could do it right away if I ask politely. I am a demon minister, after all."

I thought, *Don't conflate human priests with your demonic power*, but it sounded like the threat worked.

"I—I'm sorry! I'll do anything, so just… I'll do anything but work…"

Apparently labor didn't fall under this girl's definition of "anything"…

"Lady Beelzebub, let us hear what she has to say," the always calm and collected Fatla said smoothly. "And…I will drag my idiot little sister away from her study of the orange grave over there…"

"The orange looks so *real*!" Vania exclaimed from within the cem-etery. It sounded like a lot of trouble to have such a weird little sister…

◇

All of us entered the cramped house.

There were piles of what looked like books and games all through-out the room.

There was a table, but it was covered in a mess of things; it was almost like a hoarder's house.

"My name is Pondeli… I've been undead for almost forty years."

"I see, so you're still a newcomer," Beelzebub said.

Forty years and still a newcomer—sounds like the world of fine art.

Pondeli must have been nervous, because her cat tail was actively swishing back and forth.

"I originally lived alone in the kingdom capital, but I hated work-ing, so I always just lazed around at home. And eating was starting to become a chore, and before I knew it…I starved to death," said Pondeli.

So people out there could starve for such a shocking reason… Life sure was full of surprises…

"But I must have been mummified well, since my body didn't rot away at all. Then as I lay there, bathing in the light of the moon, I started coming to life again as an undead."

"Is it possible for something like that to happen to a dead body if it sits in the moonlight...?" I asked.

This wasn't a question a magic-user had any right to ask, but it sure was unscientific.

"The moon does have peculiar power, but that isn't enough to make a proper undead. I would imagine a mage came for an undead-making experiment when you became a corpse, no? It isn't entirely bizarre if you had that sort of help."

From what Fatla said, it sounded like it was completely possible.

"Is there anything to gain for the mage?"

"It's valuable material for experimentation. And since she was inside, they could just sneak into the room without garnering any suspicion from the townspeople."

After hearing Fatla's explanation, I finally understood. There was even demand for corpses in the world.

"And once I learned that I was undead, I didn't need to work to stay alive. I knew I had reached the pinnacle of jobless life, so now I'm wandering region to region. Oh, would you like a fruit?"

"They're practically rotten, so no thanks."

"Well, I suppose I'll take one... It might not be quite rotten yet. What a waste it would be to say no."

There was a hungry look on Beelzebub's face.

Oh right, she had some things in common with flies!

In the end, at Beelzebub's request, Pondeli placed an almost rotten—no, probably already rotten—fruit on a plate.

If someone told me this was an undead's room, I would agree.

"But back on topic, I'm now acting as graveyard watch here. I can see everything from that window. I watched one of the headstones fall over in a storm the other day."

"Given your job description, you should go put it back to normal."

"No, even if it falls, it's definitely still there, so it's fine."

"You're really just *watching*?!"

"This is a dream job. Since I'm undead, I don't get scared when I see ghosts appear."

Ah, so that was a strength of the undead.

Apparently, Pondeli would go out into the community to get some pocket change. She looked like a young girl, so some people would just give her money. And so she saved up her change to buy games and books.

Games meaning board games and card games.

"I'm the innocent type, so they must be letting me get away with it."

Don't say that yourself, I thought, but I knew what she wanted to say. This Pondeli girl was insanely laid-back.

People who owned cats didn't have them to put them to work. They were perfectly content watching them do whatever they wanted. There was a part of this girl that was like that.

"I am content with this lifestyle. Well, if there was something I didn't have..." Pondeli turned a sad gaze to the mountain of games behind her. "I'm alone most of the time, so I don't have anyone to play with. There are children who come to play sometimes, but..."

It sounded like the life of a lonely NEET was rough.

"Even with kids to play with... Everyone grows up, you know? So they go out to work or go off to get married... And then they stop coming over. That makes me sad, so I search for a different community and move there. I've done this over and over."

Pondeli's ears drooped.

"The only ones who stay kids forever are special beings like you."

Though there was a small number of immortal and near-immortal beings in this world, they were of many different kinds and races. Witches like me and demons were the same, too.

On the other hand, there were also people who grew and aged normally.

It was so hard to watch people I knew die when I first experienced it. I had to detach myself in order to keep going.

The girl said it had been about forty years since she became undead, so she still wasn't used to an immortal lifestyle. And yet all her young playmates would grow up into adults very quickly, so all she experienced was parting over and over again. This was probably the most difficult time period for her.

"What, is that all?" Fighsly said like it was no big deal. She must have had some sort of solution. "You'll never get lonely if you temper your body!"

What a stupid answer!

"Then your muscles are your friends! Ha-ha-ha!"

It'd be cruel to make her live a life where her only friends are her muscles!

"Even if what Fighsly says is rubbish, I agree that it's not too bad."

Beelzebub spoke with the generosity of someone who had lived a long time.

"So then why don't we play a game together here and now? We at least have a good number of people here."

When she said that, Beelzebub truly looked like a good older sister. This girl knew when to give up.

"There are plenty of people who would play games in the demon lands. From now on, you will be able to play games to your heart's content whenever you have free time."

"Really?! You would do that for me?!"

"I am a demon minister. It's a simple task for me, really."

Beelzebub flashed her teeth in a grin.

"Boss, you're so cool!"

"Exactly what I expect from you, Lady Beelzebub!"

"Master!"

Beelzebub's subordinates gazed at her with respect. She was acting like a big, important person, after all.

Ah, I see. I had a lot of girls around me, too, and Beelzebub was also the core of her group.

"Then what game should we play? I have so many kinds!"

"Why don't we play this Marionettes card game?"

"This is a masterpiece. You have to be so tricky, even with just a few cards! I always play this with a girl who lives in the community!"

"Playing it with just two people isn't very exciting. I recommend four to six players."

"That many people don't come here…"

And so we had a game night that lasted until morning.

Since she had so many games, we played and played with no end in sight.

It's best to have a good night's sleep, but it can be fun to cut loose every once in a while.

And as for the games themselves—

"Hmm! First place."

Beelzebub was practically unrivaled.

"Boss, I think if you went a little easier, then the games would be better from a balancing standpoint…"

"What are you talking about, Vania? Wouldn't the game be spoiled for everyone if you clearly knew that I was going easy on you? Games are battles of the mind. How rude it would be not to do it to my utmost?"

I understood what Beelzebub was getting at, but it got boring when she was number one in everything.

And Vania never failed to take last place.

It looked like the ranking of our smarts was manifesting in the results.

"Then why don't we play a game with a stronger element of luck? That game over there, Headhunters, is a sort of nonsense game."

"Wait, you can't explain the game when it's not your house."

Oh no, Beelzebub is taking over… She's acting like she owns the whole place…

Either way.

I could tell right away that Pondeli was having a fantastic time.

"I'll take first place next time!"

Both demons and cats were night owls. I just concentrated on going along with the party.

And so dawn broke.

"Phew, that was so much fun!"

"I wanted to win at least once…"

Beelzebub's near-constant victories and Vania's near-constant losses were creating two very different moods.

"Thank you all so much!"

Pondeli's expression was so lively, it was impossible to think of her as a NEET.

"Please come again. You have to! And you can bring other demons, too!"

"Certainly. In a way, we'll be closer than ever."

"What, you're moving to the area?!"

Like Pondeli, I didn't exactly know what she meant at first.

"No. You will be moving to the demon lands from here."

And that's when I remembered our original goal.

If we left the undead alone, humans might find out what she really was and dispose of her.

We had been looking for her in order to protect her.

"So for now, we shall have you live in Vanzeld town. I'm sure you will make friends there, and you can play as many games as you want on your time off."

"Huh? Time off...? That concept only applies if there will be time spent working, right...?"

"Yes. We'll have you working hard in Vanzeld town. We have simple work for you, so you'll be all right."

When Pondeli heard Beelzebub's words, her face blanched.

Then, she clung to the table.

"No! I won't work! If I have to, then I'll watch a graveyard or something! I'll do my best!"

"Fool! One day, when you're discovered to be undead, you'll be erased from this world! It would be best for you to move to demon lands and work there!" Beelzebub tugged at Pondeli's back.

"I don't mind moving, but why does a job have to come with it?!"

"Because it's part of *my* job to make sure the undead I bring in gets hired! I shan't allow something so terrible as unemployment after I've brought you in!"

"But I'd actually prefer that! I don't ever have to work!"

In a way, things were getting more complicated...

I had foreseen the two values clashing.

On the one hand, Beelzebub's values dictated, *We will protect you, so in return you will work as a proper member of society.*

On the other hand, Pondeli's was, *I don't want to work, so I won't! I have the freedom not to!*

Which was right…?

For me, who died a corporate slave, I wanted to say there was no need to force her to work.

But that probably meant that all she had to do was find a job that didn't push her.

I felt like that view wouldn't validate someone who refused to do any work at all, too. Nobody around me insisted on life as a NEET in the first place.

Beelzebub's intentions probably weren't compulsory labor; she probably just thought that a member of society should work for a profession to earn money to live.

At least that much was true. Humans were creatures who participated in society through work…

But was it okay to force someone who refused to work?

"You will not earn any money if you do not work! You won't be able to live!"

"Yes, I will! I'm undead so I don't need to eat! I'm perfectly content with receiving fruit or whatever from people who want to indulge me once in a while!"

"That's not what makes an independent adult!"

"I have no plans to be independent, but I'm not causing trouble for my parents, either!"

Fighsly and Fatla looked on in bewilderment.

"Um, Miss Azusa? What should we do about this?"

"Fighsly, you handed this off to me at the right time… So, what do you think about this? The questioner should give her opinion first."

"To be honest, I want to be rich, so I don't understand the mentality of refusing work itself."

"You money-grubbing woman!"

"Money-grubbing slime, actually. Motivating myself with money makes life even more fun, and it's easier to set goals."

I guess that was how a freelancer might think about it, too. There were countless answers out there in the world.

"Thank you, Fighsly. Now, what do you think, Fatla?"

"For me, I believe she should move to Vanzeld Castle normally and work. Because if she stays here, we don't know when she'll be discovered as an undead and be put down. She should not live a jobless existence that puts her life in danger."

"That's reasonable."

It was weird for an undead's "life" to be in danger, though.

"Then you're the last, Azusa."

Tch. Now they're asking for my opinion outright.

"Indeed, indeed. Azusa, tell us what you think!"

"The demons are turning employment into too much of a virtue! As a human representative, please tell them about the significance of not working!"

The bickering duo looked to me.

Urgh... It's sounding like my opinion is going to decide everything...

I wonder if there's some sort of magic that could produce good advice... Of course not...

"A-ahem..."

All right, I'll make this work somehow with my own words.

"Oh, though I wouldn't mind should you choose to let her mooch off you in your house in the highlands."

"Nope, not happening."

"My, that was rather dry of you."

Beelzebub seemed slightly surprised at that, but we did take turns with household responsibilities, after all.

I even made my daughters help out with the cooking and cleaning. I couldn't have someone in my house who wouldn't do any of that. It would completely throw off the general mood of the household.

"Well, the answer is obvious."

Let this solve the problem!

"Pondeli should open a game lounge wherever she moves to!"

Both Beelzebub and Pondeli blinked at me.

That probably wasn't enough for them to understand, so I explained a little more.

"Pondeli, you like playing games with everyone, right?"

"Most games need a bigger number of players... I got so fired up playing with so many people, like this time around!"

"Then, this is just a guess, but I'm sure there are tons of people in the demon lands who don't have enough people to play with. So why don't you start a trade where people pay you to play games with them? Then you can play while you work."

"Azusa, is that work...? That sounds to be a bit much..."

"If it fails as a business, then it just doesn't generate any money. Since it's a one-man business, it's possible she won't make any profits, but since Pondeli doesn't really need to eat to live, it's no harm no foul, right?"

"Oh, that's right! I'll be conducting business in a legal sense, then! I might be able to do that!"

Pondeli's expression brightened. That was a good reaction.

"I see! If I get a lot of offers to play, then I can earn money by playing! And if I don't get any offers, then I don't have to work! It's a win-win!"

"Yes! I'm sure that won't be a problem for you!"

I felt oddly excited, probably because I'd stayed up all night. My brain was getting flushed with dopamine. Yeehaw!

"And so, what do you think, Beelzebub?"

"Rgh... Rrrrrgh..."

Since Beelzebub was a government official, she probably still wasn't completely satisfied with the idea, but—

"Ooh! Fine, fine! I'll put in an application for it! But you will submit a notification that you are opening a business, okay?! Otherwise I won't acknowledge your so-called 'game lounge'!"

All right! Problem solved!

"Thank you, Miss Azusa!"

Pondeli bowed her head over and over.

"It's fine; it's fine. I hope you thrive in Vanzeld town."

"Oh, but moving is going to be such a pain…"

She glanced around at the rest of us.

"That much you can do yourself!"

◇

Beelzebub paid me for helping with the investigation, and I went back to the house in the highlands.

Since I had stayed up all night, I went straight to sleep once I got home.

And I know you're asking what I used the investigation money for—

"Okay, then Falfa's going to use a defense card there. ♪"

"I won't stop you! I will use a card that strengthens my attack even more!"

"Then Shalsha will stop you with a cancelation card."

Yep—I used it to purchase a number of card and board games we could enjoy at home.

We were playing a two-versus-two card game at the moment. It was my two daughters versus Halkara and me.

"Madam Teacher, please use an extra power-up attack card here!"

"Aww, but I like it when my daughters cooperate together, so I won't."

"Oh, Madam Teacher! You should not underestimate our opponents! That doesn't make for a fun game!"

My daughters seemed really excited about the games, so they'd been playing whenever they found some free time recently.

Maybe I should implement a rule limiting game time to one hour a day soon…

"Phew, this is true nirvana!"

As I soaked in the outdoor bath, I gave a sigh of bliss.

The whole family was bathing in the hot springs at the volcano in Laika's hometown.

I didn't have a good grasp of how many geothermal hot spots there were in this world, but at the very least, there were several hot spring inns at the volcano, and most of them had outdoor baths.

Since it would be a waste otherwise, I visited a different inn every single time I came. But it wasn't like there were dozens of them, so I'd soon be on my second go around. I'd probably find my preferred inn to stay at before too long.

"Lady Azusa, what is nirvana?" Laika asked me. Oh right, she wouldn't understand that word.

"Well, it's like heaven. It means a place filled with the most happiness."

"I see! How informative. I knew you were so abundant in your knowledge, Lady Azusa."

But it was of course a word that any ex-Japanese person would know, so I sort of felt sorry for receiving that compliment.

"This is more hell than heaven..."

Flatorte lay flat on her stomach outside the outdoor bath.

Blue dragons apparently didn't handle heat very well, and she'd gotten out of the bath almost right away. Then Halkara started pouring water on her.

"Ooh, my body feels heavy…"

"Flatorte, you were in the bath only for about fifteen seconds. That sounds much too quick to get dizzy…"

"Yeah, I'll return to normal, then try it again…"

Well, some people couldn't handle baths very well. Even if the water wasn't all that hot.

And by the way, my two daughters weren't breaking any of our rules for manners, like splashing around and swimming. They were perfectly well-behaved. They seemed to enjoy the big bath.

"Halkara, Flatorte seems fine now, so you can come in if you want."

"Is that so? If you insist, then."

Halkara came back to the bath.

Her bosom was floating on the water.

Hmm… I always imagined elves as slender, so then what was up with Halkara's breasts?

"Big Sis Halkara, you really have big boobies!"

"Miss Halkara, when did this happen to you?"

Aah, and now my daughters are interested! But they've never asked me stuff like that before…

"Are they? Now that you mention it, there were berries at home that had something in them that increased breast size, and I ate those a lot. Maybe that's it."

She said something I couldn't ignore.

"Halkara, we're going to go pick those berries next time!"

"Huh?! Really, Madam Teacher?"

"Really, really! If I can get this strong defeating slimes for three hundred years, then I'm sure the effects would be incredible if I ate those berries for thirty years!"

—And putting that aside.

"Ooh, the water was so nice!"

We changed after we got out of the bath and left the dressing rooms. What I wore wasn't my usual clothes but my pajamas.

Well, I'm not Flatorte, but I guess I should cool off somewhere. Still, the spring was in a volcano, so it was hot even outside the bath.

Then, to the left of the changing room exit, a door that said GAME ROOM on it caught my attention.

"Game room? Do they really have games here?"

I guess hot spring inns in the suburbs often had old shooting games in them. Maybe it was the same here. But there probably wouldn't be any arcade cabinets.

"Games? Yay, sounds fun!"

Falfa opened the door right away.

Sitting there wasn't an arcade cabinet, obviously, but it was still something I recognized well.

It was a table with a net in the middle.

Could this be…?

"Oh, it's a pin-pone table," Laika said.

"I knew it was Ping-Pong!"

"Pin-pone is a very well-known sport among the dragons. Blue dragons play it a lot, too," Flatorte said.

I didn't know why, but there was no question that dragons played Ping-Pong.

"You may not know about it, Lady Azusa, so I'll explain the rules. We use this pin-pone seed that's hollow on the inside as a ball, and both players hit it back and forth with rackets. So when you serve, you bounce it once on your side of the court, then hit it with—"

"Oh yeah, I get the gist of it. Actually, you could say I'm experienced."

It matched the rules for Ping-Pong one for one. I didn't know if it totally matched up with world conference regulations, but the basics were exactly the same.

"It sounds like you know the game, Lady Azusa, so why don't we have a match while we're here? Both rackets and balls are in the basket."

Laika brought over the Ping-Pong equipment (*I'm just going to call it Ping-Pong*) from the corner of the room.

"All right, let's do this! Hot springs and Ping-Pong always go hand in hand!"

"No, Lady Azusa, it's pin-pone."

She corrected me, but I was just going to stick to Ping-Pong.

The racket was exactly the same as a regular Ping-Pong one. There was even a rubberlike substance stuck to it. But it seemed like all they had were the double-faced ones.

The first match was between Laika and me.

"I won't lose, Laika! I'll show you the dignity of the head of the house!"

Laika was the first to serve.

I may not look it, but I was once a part of a Ping-Pong club called Curve that made it its goal to play Ping-Pong at hot springs. The name came from the curved arc the ball went in.

It would be cheeky of me to count myself as an experienced player, but I wasn't exactly a beginner.

Laika tossed the ball in the air. It was coming straight to my side of the court.

I went at the ball with my racket.

"Ha!"

But the ball flew straight past the table and into next week.

"Wha…? This is pretty tough…"

"The first point goes to me. Let's go again."

The ball flew at me once more. I swung my racket.

This time the ball went straight into the net.

"…Hey, Laika, you're putting a spin on the ball, aren't you?"

"Yes. Adding a spin to your serve is a basic tactic, of course," Laika said, her expression suggesting it was the obvious thing to do.

Aww, come on. Isn't it mean to take hot spring Ping-Pong this seriously? Aren't we supposed to be exchanging lighter hits?

Which, by the way, I couldn't do.

"I'm sure you may have your own thoughts about this, but I will not go easy on you. That would be much too rude to my opponent."

She was as sharp as always, but to have Ping-Pong at a hot springs be the motivation for it…

"Oh well. I guess I'll just have to step up to the plate now, huh?"

1–11

I got my butt handed to me.

There wasn't much I could do anyway, since my opponent got all the points when it was her serve. When I got lucky and got the ball in her court, it was high and easy to hit, so she just struck it way far out…

All my serves had high bounces, so she hit them straight back to me with a strong arm.

I remembered when Beelzebub took all the games seriously when we were playing at Pondeli's place. Sure, it wasn't good to go easy when playing cerebral games, but when it came to sports, it wouldn't be a good game without a handicap…

"All right, would anyone else like to play?"

Laika seemed to be having fun. *That's not very grown-up at all! Well, body size doesn't make her an adult, though.*

Afterward, Falfa and Shalsha stepped up to the challenge, but since they didn't even know the rules, they lost without taking a single point.

Rosalie, who was a ghost and couldn't even get in the hot springs, also easily lost. I mean, she couldn't handle the racket well enough to hit the ball, so what could she do? I wanted to praise her just for managing to play a game.

Halkara was also a beginner, so she wasn't very good, but there was a bigger problem with her.

Her bosom looked like it was going to pop out of her pajamas whenever she moved, so I stepped in during the middle of the match.

"Okay, stop! This is too risky! I can't say for sure that a male guest isn't going to come into this room at any time… You should be more discreet about that…"

"I'm sorry. My chest is in the way, which makes it hard to use the racket."

I was getting extremely irritated by my own personal feelings.

In the end, Laika was undefeated.

It felt cheap, like a member of the Ping-Pong club was playing with a bunch of casuals.

"All right, perhaps I should switch with someone soon."

"Wait! One of us hasn't tried yet—Flatorte!"

Flatorte stuck out her right hand and stepped up to the challenge.

"Very well. Actually, I believe this match will come to a quick conclusion."

"My strategy was to tire you out by making you play against everyone else."

Flatorte was petty, too!

"I'm sorry, but it's impossible to return my serves with the spin I put on the ball."

"Then go ahead and try. I have a secret technique."

Whether she actually had any secret techniques or not, there was no questioning Flatorte was raring to go.

"Here we go!"

Laika tossed the ball up high and brushed it with her racket.

She put a spin on it this time, too!

Then, Flatorte—

"*Roooaaar!* Here it comes!"

—practically smashed the ball back into Laika's court.

Laika couldn't even begin to match that energy. To think Flatorte was starting out ahead!

"Wow, amazing!" "You did it, Miss Flatorte!" "That was a full-body hit."

My daughters and I yelled practically all at the same time!

"I—I see! She can deal with the serve by adding even more of a spin on her return hit!"

Halkara sounded like an expository character when she spoke. But it was an easy-to-understand explanation.

"I, Flatorte, don't really understand that stuff about spins. But a spin naturally occurs when I swing my racket. I'm overwriting Laika's spin entirely with my own!"

To me, it sounded like a technique that just used force, but it was effective, so I guessed it was fine.

"Impressive. But I haven't even started yet. You didn't think I was just planning on winning through my serves, did you?"

Oh, the color in Laika's eyes changed.

This is gonna be an intense fight...

"All right then, come at me!"

Their match quickly turned into a melee.

It was hard to tell if it was skill or just pure energy, but whenever Laika served, Flatorte would always hit it right back.

Of course, that didn't knock Laika off her game, and she was fielding it well.

And Flatorte was keeping up, always smacking it right back with an aggressive stance.

This is getting exciting...

Flatorte's attack sometimes failed and Laika earned a point, but there were also plenty of times when it entered Flatorte's court and then shot straight past Laika.

The game was complicated right up until the last phase.

16–16

A deuce wouldn't settle the matter.

How will it turn out...?

We watched with bated breath to see where this was going.

"I see sweat on Miss Laika's cheek that wasn't there at the beginning. I believe she might not have much left in her."

Halkara was right at home explaining to the audience, wasn't she…?

"Big Sis Halkara, is Big Sis Flatorte at an advantage?"

"It's not that simple, little Falfa. This is a hot springs in a volcano. With the high temperatures, a blue dragon like Flatorte will be at a disadvantage when it comes to long battles. In actuality, she's been making more mistakes since the second half started."

It was a mystery as to why Halkara, who supposedly had never played this game before, could provide such an accurate analysis. My mind was on the match, but now it was also on that…

"This match will come to an end soon."

Halkara the explainer's opinion became reality.

"Hey, Laika, let's get rid of the two-point advantage and say whoever gets the next single point wins."

Laika would be serving next, so Flatorte offered a suggestion.

"Are you sure? Don't blame me if you regret it."

"You're the one who'll decide if I'll catch this one."

Laika nodded slowly.

A drop of sweat fell to the floor.

"Very well. I'll end this with my next serve."

"Heh, and I'll return it!"

Then, Laika grinned.

"Actually, I have a secret serving technique that I haven't shown once yet."

"Whatever serve it may be, I, the great Flatorte, will send it right back! Even if your technique is better than mine, my game sense isn't to be underestimated!"

Things were getting heated. This didn't feel like hot spring Ping-Pong…

"Technique versus instinct—a clash of dragon pride. Now, what sort of serve will we see next?"

"Halkara, Laika should naturally have the advantage, since she'll be using a new move here. What do you think about that?"

"Well, at this point this is a battle of pride, so it's hard to say how much of an effect it'll have. Flatorte would be able to push back against a tricky serve with her power!"

For some reason I really wanted to read a sports manga, whether about Ping-Pong or tennis or something else. Unfortunately, they didn't exist in this world.

"Then this serve will end it all! I will never allow you to receive!"

"Enough talk—just hit the ball!"

The ball slowly rose into the air.

Then Laika moved in a way I had never seen before.

She was holding the racket vertically, like she was going to chop the ball in half.

"Here we go!"

Laika swung the racket at high speed!

And without even touching the ball, it sliced through empty air.

The ball plopped down.

"I—I—I... I won!!!"

Flatorte took on a victorious pose in celebration. Something about this felt unfinished, but there was no questioning she won.

"I beat a red dragon! I beat a red dragon!"

Logically, that was correct, but that phrasing made it sound like it meant something different!

"W-wait! Deciding the winner like that will only leave a bad taste in both our mouths, so we should just do it normally with a two-point advantage!"

Laika, you're sounding childish!

"Hmm? The great Flatorte won fair and square. No need to play anymore!"

Flatorte was smug as sin. She could look as smug as she wanted today. She had won convincingly.

"Then, then... One more match! Let us have one more match!"

Laika was such a sore loser! She really did take everything seriously.

"No. Actually, I'll never play with you again. That way, Flatorte's victory will forever remain etched in history!"

And Flatorte was really petty about this stuff!

Afterward, since the two of them worked up quite a sweat, we all went back into the baths for another soak.

In the water, Laika was still asking Flatorte for a rematch.

"Sheesh, will you cut it out already? No need to obsess over something so trivial!" I scolded.

"How dare you! I have my regrets!"

Next time, we'll stay at an inn without a Ping-Pong table...

I made a vow to myself as I soaked in the water.

In the morning, as always, the family gathered in the dining room.

Today was Halkara's turn to make food, so there were generally lots of vegetables.

In cooking, everyone's personalities showed themselves. Laika used a lot of eggs in her cooking, and Flatorte always made rich meat dishes, even in the morning.

When I cooked, I thought my meals were comparatively balanced, but I wasn't actually sure.

At the very least, it was much better than the *orange juice and done!* kinds of breakfasts I had when I was a corporate slave. Whether it was "feminine" or "masculine" wasn't the issue; it was just hard on my humanity.

"Oh, Rosalie isn't here today," Halkara said, gazing up at the ceiling.

Even though she was a ghost and didn't eat anything, Rosalie was usually floating near the ceiling, just enjoying the company of her family.

"Lack of sleep? But I suppose *sleep* isn't really a thing for her."

Since she was dead, Rosalie led a life without what we'd call our three basic needs. It must be hell for a ghost to see such tantalizing food without being able to eat it like she wanted, so I thought she was doing well in that department.

I decided to call for her.

"Rosalie, where are you?"

It was like calling out for a house cat, but Rosalie was much easier to lose track of.

No response.

She wasn't above me or below me.

I peeked into the rooms on the first floor and the wide shared space in the wooden extension that Laika built, but she wasn't there, either.

Her absence started to worry me…

I headed for Rosalie's room on the second floor. Rosalie wasn't disadvantaged by having to physically go upstairs, so she used the second floor.

The door opened with a *clack*, but she wasn't there.

Her personal stuffed dogs and cats were there, and that was all. She liked stuffed animals, so she would save up her allowance and buy them sometimes.

"Huh? If she's not here, then where did she go…? I mean, she can go to Flatta or Nascúte or wherever…"

And when I was about to leave the room—

"Big Sis, Big Sis! I'm here!"

I heard Rosalie's voice.

But it sounded a little different than usual, almost slightly muffled.

And I still couldn't see where she was.

"Hey, Rosalie, where on earth are you? I can't tell where you are when you just say *here*!"

She was definitely close by, so I gazed around the room.

That's when I noticed it.

At one spot on the wall, the wooden textures looked like a ghastly face.

"*Aaaah!* It's haunted! Like something from a horror flick!"

Monsters and spirits and stuff didn't scare me after all this time. Demons came by the house pretty often, after all.

But I could *not* handle hauntings and unexplained phenomena! It gave me the shivers! And goose bumps!

I have to run! I have to get out of here now!

"Big Sis, wait! It's me!"

Rosalie's voice echoed around me again. And it somehow sounded like it was coming from…

"Hey! Don't scare me like that! That's you, right, Rosalie?!"

"Yes… I had a little accident…"

I guess once Rosalie got caught in the wall, a terrifying visage appeared. Was this another part of a ghost's power…?

"Whatever, just come out right now. This is terrible for my heart."

"Well… I can't…" The wall sounded embarrassed.

"Huh? Isn't it a piece of cake for a ghost to slip through walls?"

"Actually, I was just sitting here for a bit. Then, for some reason, I got caught and couldn't move…"

Was something so bizarre possible? But, I guess it was happening in real life…

I had no idea what to do about this on my own, so I called the whole family in (except Halkara, who had gone to work at the factory).

But no one could think of a quick fix.

Not only was it the rarest of cases, but none of us had been ghosts before.

Shalsha brought in dictionaries from her room and started looking up words.

I didn't think that would solve anything, but it would be bad for her education if I told her outright that it wouldn't work, so I just watched.

"I learned that *stuck in a wall* was an old idiomatic expression."

"Huh, and what does it mean?"

Was it maybe a phenomenon that had happened a lot in the olden days? Ghosts themselves had been around forever, after all.

"It means—nothing can be done. To be at a loss. A situation where giving up is the only solution."

"Okay, that's not helping!"

Whoops, I ended up shooting her down…

"As the one who built this part of the house, I'm loath to suggest it, but why don't we break the wall here? Rosalie may be able to get out then."

Laika offered an aggressive, dragon-like solution.

Before I could say anything, Rosalie resisted. "That's scary, so don't do it! I might be cut into tiny pieces!" I couldn't say for sure there was no risk, so I agreed.

"What if you space out again and end up slipping out? That's how I, Flatorte, have lived life so far."

Flatorte's ideas didn't deviate much from one another...

But sometimes things just come off by the time you've forgotten about them, more often than you think. Like when you go back to open a lid on a bottle and it comes right off even though it was stuck the first time.

"By the way, Rosalie, how do you feel right now?"

"If I had to describe it... Nothingness."

Her response sounded vaguely religious.

"It's been a while since I died, but this is the emptiest I've felt. Futility, maybe, or nihility... I want to get out of here soon..."

I guess we couldn't just leave her.

"All right! Falfa will push you out!"

Falfa rolled up her already short sleeves—

—breathed in slowly—

—and rammed right into the wooden wall. *Bam!*

Whoa! That was a full-bodied blow!

As a result of that...

"Waaah, ow, oww! My arms feel tingly..."

I saw it coming, but Falfa just got hurt.

"Aww, Falfa, you should think carefully about doing something before you do it, okay?"

She was still a child, so I wanted her to be more thoughtful at times like this. I looked at Falfa's arm.

"Are you bleeding? There's no blood. Good, good."

I stroked Falfa's arm.

"This'll make the pain go away. Pain, pain, go away!"

"Wow, Mommy, that's incredible! I think it actually hurts less! You're like a magician, Mommy!"

I've been a witch for three hundred years, by the way.

Whether or not it actually had any effect, Falfa stopped crying, so that was good enough for me.

—But then, I got an idea.

I slowly stood before Rosalie (and the wall she was in).

I gently brushed the wall, stroking it back and forth with my right hand.

"Ah-ha-ha! Ha-ha-ha-ha-ha!! Stop, Big Sis! That tickles!"

The voice came from the wall in response.

It was working, but it was unclear if it would help her get out.

"You know, I noticed we hadn't touched the wall at all. Since you melded with it, I wondered if it would tickle you if I touched it," I said as my hands continued to stroke the wall.

Anyone just looking on might think I was being perverse, but I was super serious about this.

"Gyah! Ee-hee-hee… Ah-ha-ha-ha-ha… Stop, stop! I'm gonna die…!"

"You're fine! You're already dead!"

Her reaction was promising. And it was getting more and more effective.

Wouldn't giving the wall a good rub like this bring her out of it?

If she didn't—well, we'd cross that bridge when we came to it! We had nothing to lose!

"Everyone, pet the wall with me! Like you're tickling it!"

My two daughters, Laika, and Flatorte all lined up with me and started lightly touching the wall.

"Yaaa-haaaaaaa! Wah-ha-ha-ha! I can't do this anymore! This is hell, hell! Eeeeee! Yaaaaaa!"

Rosalie sure was cracking up. *Now come on out!*

"I can't take it anymore!!!"

Then, suddenly, Rosalie popped out from the wall.

Her eyes were watering, even though she was a ghost. Maybe it really was ticklish for her.

"Sheesh! You guys went way too far! I've never been tortured like that before!"

"But we succeeded in getting you out, right?"

Rosalie looked around to see where she was.

"Oh, you're right... I didn't think that would work..."

And so Rosalie's ensnarement in the wall was solved peacefully, and she never spaced out in a wall again.

We all needed to be careful not to trap ourselves between a wall and a hard place.

When I woke up in the morning, breakfast wasn't ready yet.

I checked to see if it was my turn that day and I forgot, but it wasn't. I thought that maybe Halkara had a drink before bed and ended up sleeping in (which had happened in the past), but it wasn't her day, either.

Right. It was definitely Laika's day.

I repeatedly knocked on the door to Laika's room.

After a little while, Laika flew out of the room in her fancy pajamas.

"My apologies, Lady Azusa! I will start breakfast at once!"

From the looks of it, she overslept.

That was unusual for her, but people did oversleep at least once or twice in their lives. It wasn't like she was late for work or anything, so it wasn't a big deal.

"Oh, no rush. No one else is up yet but me, so take your time getting ready."

"No! One's routine will fall apart if one makes too many allowances! I will begin my preparations right away!"

Still in her pajamas, Laika stood in the kitchen cutting the ham, whisking the eggs, and starting her breakfast.

She would insist on doing things her way when she got like this, so I read a grimoire as I waited.

"All right! This is ham and eggs with a drizzle of ketchup on top!"

"Oh, it's a simple meal, but Falfa and Shalsha will be delighted to eat it." My daughters were children, so they liked things sweetened with ketchup. "All right, I'm going to dig in, then."

"I am so very sorry for making you wait!"

Hmm, it sort of felt like she was prioritizing diligence a little too much again.

It probably wasn't actually that big of a change, since it depended on the personality, but I just decided to mention it.

"Hey, I'm not a guest, so you don't have to be all fired up about this. Why not take it easier? It's harder to break something flexible."

"B-but there's a difference between that and skipping my— Ha, ah, ah, ah…"

Then, Laika's mouth opened in an odd way. And just as it occurred to me, *Hey, her expression is really strange—*

"Chooooooooooooooo!!!!!"

An explosive tempest of a sneeze came from her mouth.

The plate that I was about to eat from almost flew away, so I managed to just catch the plate itself. The food scattered all over the table, so I put everything back on the plates as fast as I could for the three-second rule.

That aside.

"Uh, Laika? You weren't sleeping in because you had a cold, were you?"

Anyone would think so if they saw that sneeze.

I guess I could also be thankful that flames hadn't come out of her mouth.

"Oh, no, I'm just a little under the weather… Ah, ah, ah…"

Since I'd borne the brunt of it just now, I used my experience to get right up close to Laika and cover her mouth with my hand. I somehow made it in time.

"Mumble, mumble…"

Oh, it'd be hard for her to breathe if I kept it closed all the time. I drew my hand away.

"I—I'm sorry, Lady Azusa…"

"Stay put. I'll take your temperature."

I put my hand right onto Laika's forehead.

"Ack! That's a real fever right there! It's *way* too hot, actually! I'm surprised you're still alive…"

The sensation was like holding a cup filled with hot tea.

"I think that's because I'm a red dragon… My body temperature is high to begin with…"

Okay. I guess we go with the dragon rules instead of the human rules here.

Even so, it was a sure thing that she had a cold.

"Laika, go back to your room and sleep. I'll take care of everyone's breakfast."

"B-but…"

I scooped Laika up to carry her in my arms.

"I *really* hate it when people who aren't healthy force themselves to work. It's dangerous if it gets any worse, it's inefficient, and if someone unwell can't afford to take a shift off, then the guy who put the shifts together is incompetent! Now sleep!"

I carried Laika and forced her into her bed.

Then I put ice and water and cold towels and stuff on her, but they all dried up very quickly. Her temperature was really high…

"Let me ask just in case, but are there any life-threatening illnesses that only dragons can catch?"

"Dragons are hardy, so no… Ha*choo*, I think I got too cold while I was sleeping… The highlands are cooler than the volcano, after all…"

For me, the highland air was refreshing and felt great, but it sounded like Laika's thoughts on the matter were different.

"Then rest a lot today. You can help out as much as you want once you've recovered. I will *really* be upset if you force yourself up or if you pass your cold on to any other family members. Right now, your duty is to recover from your cold, okay? That's all!"

If I didn't decisively tell her to rest, then she would leave her room again.

I could dote on her after she'd slept for a while. I had to be Laika's substitute for the day.

I asked Shalsha about Laika's symptoms when she woke up, and she told me it was an illness with the very straightforward name of "dragon cold."

"It's not serious, but the greatest symptom displayed is a sneeze strong enough to blow things away."

"Yep, I've experienced that. I guess it's pretty typical."

Then all we had to do was make sure she got better.

"Madam Teacher, times like these call for Nutri-Spirits, don't they?"

"No! We can't have her feeling like she wants to work anymore!"

I shot down Halkara's idea.

That being said, she did have a brain for medicine, so I guess I could ask her to help.

"Halkara, can you take today off from the factory?"

"Yes. I'm the president, so I may do what I like."

"Go out and pick several kinds of herbs. In the meantime, I'll watch over her."

It was times like these that the whole family working together could make a difference.

"Flatorte, make some ice. Rosalie, Falfa, Shalsha, do the cleaning in Laika's place today."

Now that I was done assigning jobs, I put my heart and soul into nursing Laika back to health.

Laika's forehead was still burning up, so it felt like she was gravely ill, but it was just a cold. The room was stuffy from the heat, but sweating was good for you when you were sick. That was probably no big deal.

What I needed to be careful of was that her sweat didn't cool her down too much when she slept.

"Okay, we're changing clothes, Laika."

"I—I'm sorry, Lady Azusa…"

Every two hours or so, I would have Laika remove her clothes and put on new ones.

She was sweating way more than a human, so I had to take thorough care of her.

"These sorts of colds typically go away within the day, so you don't have to worry so much…"

"Huh. Perfect, then." I looked at her with confidence. "You ask for whatever you want today. Laika, you're always trying to do things on your own, you know."

Laika's face was already red from her fever, but it looked like it got even redder.

"Understood…"

I knew that Laika was really a spoiled girl. But her education hid that by cultivating the parts of her that made her a stable individual. Think of a businessman whining, "Mommy, it's too stifling…," and not getting on the train to work in the morning. Everyone ends up molded into proper people.

But being proper all the time was definitely too stifling.

A balloon continually filled with air would burst. The act of depleting some of that air was necessary.

Before long, Laika was sleeping soundly. It didn't seem like she was having a nightmare, so maybe she was getting better.

But then, she murmured something in her sleep.

"Elder Sister…"

Her big sister had gotten married. I know I said it before, but I had to be her pseudo–big sister.

Working so expeditiously for my younger sister…made me sleepy, too.

I sat on the bed and figured a five-minute snooze should be okay. *Yeah, five minutes will be fine…*

I woke up when I realized someone was petting my head.

It was Laika, sitting up in bed.

"Oh! Lady Azusa… You're awake?"

She was surprised when I opened my eyes. I sat up.

"Sorry, I guess I fell asleep while I was watching over you. I hope I didn't get in your way, though."

"It was not a problem at all. Thank you for looking after me. It seems like my fever has gone down as well."

"I see. This is all because of your *big sister*'s care."

I deliberately emphasized *big sister*.

Laika's right hand gently covered her mouth. Her ears were red, so that probably meant she was embarrassed.

"Ever since your big sister, Leila, got married, you've had less people you can lean on, right? I decided on the day of her wedding that I would take her place. You laid your head on my lap that day, didn't you?"

"Y-yes… I remember it well…"

It sounded like Laika still remembered that. She quickly nodded.

"From now on, you can be the little sister you want to be, as much as you want to be. Growing up doesn't mean you have to stop depending on others. If you need to lean on me, then do it. If you don't, then I'll indulge you myself."

"Growing up does not mean discarding all dependencies… There is weight to those words. I will make a note of this later."

She was probably planning on avoiding the whole thing by saying something so stiff.

But I guess that was fine. My feelings got through to her anyway. She was my little sister, after all.

"But why were you petting me?"

My memory was hazy, but it felt like she had run her hand over my hair a number of times.

Laika's expression grew hesitant, and she looked away.

Wait, is there really a problem here?

"Well… Lady Azusa, you looked very cute when you were sleeping… Like a little sister…," she said, still averting her eyes.

"I wanted to be the older sister, but now I'm the younger one?!"

What was up with that? My scheme had lost the plot!

"Certainly, you're normally like my…a big sister, Lady Azusa. But your sleeping face looked much younger than I thought… And if you look younger than me when you are sleeping…it's very much like a little sister tired out from caring for the sick then falling asleep…"

She's not following along at all!

Could it be that I was the only one who was planning on being the older sister? Am I getting complacent…?

"I'm sorry! You are very much like an older sister to me, Lady Azusa! I don't often think of you as a younger sister!"

But you do sometimes.

"Then the next time I catch a cold, you'll take care of me, right, *Big Sis Laika*?"

"Please do not tease me like that, Lady Azusa!"

"Big Sis Laika, you don't have to speak so formally to your little sister."

"Please, stop with this!"

Afterward, I created a bitter medicine from the herbs Halkara picked. When I made Laika drink it, her cold got all better.

The End

©Benio

It's been a while. This is Kisetsu Morita!

There is a lot of information I need to announce since the second volume, so I'll start with that!

First, we've decided to put out a drama CD! Ta-daa!

Of course, I can't announce the voice-acting cast, but the on-sale date has been decided. It will be January next year! So, in six months. I would be very happy if you sit tight and wait patiently!

Also, since there are a great number of characters in this work, no matter what, having every character appear won't happen unless I turn into an oil magnate and invest a lot of money into it. So I'm thinking about doing a story with a scene after the festival that happened at the beginning of Volume 2.

Next, serial publication of the comic version has begun in *Gan-Gan GA*!

I would be delighted if you would enjoy seeing Azusa's world drawn by Yusuke Shiba-sensei! I am incredibly excited to see how the author will develop things in the future!

This is especially so, since Shiba-sensei previously drew a comedy about a witch. I think he is the perfect casting choice for *I've Been Killing Slimes for 300 Years...*, etc.

Also, in *GanGan GA*, where the comic version is being published, I've started serializing a spin-off story about Beelzebub!

As of now, the starting schedule hasn't been set yet, but I think it will start either just before or right after this book comes out.

I know it's a little late to say this, but *I've Been Killing Slimes for 300 Years...* is written from the first-person view of the main character, Azusa.

So I can't show what the characters are doing in environments that Azusa isn't present in.

And so, it was the perfect opportunity to focus on the life of Beelzebub, who is in the position of agriculture minister—essentially the minister for agriculture and forestry. As anyone could imagine, she had a lot happen to her before she became minister...

I'm hoping to dig deeper into the stories of Beelzebub and her subordinate leviathans, Fatla and Vania, since they aren't talked about much in the main story.

Regarding serialization, we are planning on publishing twice every month (which is the general rate for *GanGan GA*. And each one will be about four times the volume of main stories published in *So You Want to Be a Novelist*).

I hope you will read this, too!

I'll pop the *GanGan GA* URL here!
http://www.ganganonline.com/contents/slime/

All right, now we can finally talk about Volume 3!

That being said, it's a little pointless for someone who's already read it...

I introduced a lot of new characters in Volume 3. Flatorte (who was already around, but she got a picture in Volume 3), Fighsly, Eno, Pondeli. When I put them all together, I noticed they're all problem children... But I would be delighted if you showed these girls some love, too.

I wrote about this back in Volume 1, but this story is about a slow-paced life that centers on Azusa.

Azusa is living a laid-back life her own way, but I think a hundred people would have many different ways to take it easy.

I'm hoping to represent all those different kinds of relaxing life-styles through different characters.

Those reading the serialization in *So You Want to Be a Novelist* might already know this, but these characters will pop up again here and there and start getting involved with Azusa and her family. I want to write about a world slowly becoming linked by friends from all sorts of different lands.

And this time also includes three bonus episodes! I hope you've enjoyed getting to see the appeal of some characters who I haven't been able to show in the main story!

Now, I have nothing but thanks for Benio-sensei, who has breathed life into so many characters. I am so happy to see the cuteness coming out of the characters, even when they're deformed!

Especially Flatorte, who's oozing with that cuteness unique to dumb little kids. It's great. I would love to do nothing but make fried rice and *yakisoba* and stuff and give it to girls like her (weird desire, I know).

And I give my deepest, deepest thanks to all those who've purchased this third volume. To express how I feel in one word about a story I started out writing as a pure hobby now being turned into a comic, drama CD, and various media like this, and then getting spread to people—pure joy. And the whole reason this has been possible is because of everyone who has been purchasing these books. Thank you so much!

Also, *The Mysterious Job Called Oda Nobunaga* is on sale at the same time as this book! It's a battle tale that's of a different breed than slimes, so I hope you'll take a look at that, too!

I'll see you again in Volume 4!

Kisetsu Morita